2012
TUSCANY PRIZE
FOR
CATHOLIC FICTION

Selected

Short

Stories

TUSCANY
PRESS LLC

WELLESLEY, MASSACHUSETTS
www.TuscanyPress.com

Tuscany Press, LLC
Wellesley, Massachusetts
www.TuscanyPress.com

Peter J. Mongeau is the Founder and Publisher of Tuscany Press, LLC.

Publisher's Cataloging-in-Publication Data
(Prepared by The Donohue Group, Inc.)

2012 Tuscany Prize for Catholic Fiction : selected short stories / [Joseph O'Brien, editor].

    p. ; cm.

    Issued also as an ebook.
    ISBN: 978-1-939627-03-2 (hardcover)
    ISBN: 978-1-939627-04-9 (pbk.)

    1. Catholic fiction. 2. Short stories--Catholic authors. I. O'Brien, Joseph (Joseph Leo), 1969- II. Title: Selected short stories

PN6120.92.C38 A13 2013
808.839/921/282   2013930519

Printed and bound in the United State of America

10   9 8 7 6 5 4 3 2 1

Text design and layout by Peri Swan
This book was typeset in Garamond Premier Pro with Shelley Andante Script as a display typeface.

Contents

Preface

We at Tuscany Press have been asked many times: Why Tuscany Press, why Catholic fiction, and why a Catholic short story collection?

Let me start by inviting you into the world of Catholic readers as we have experienced it. We noticed that if we wanted to read good Catholic fiction, we had to reach back to the writers of the last century: Flannery O'Conner, Walker Percy, Graham Greene, and then further back to J. R. R. Tolkien and G. K. Chesterton. Look as we might it seemed as if good contemporary Catholic fiction did not exist.

We asked ourselves how that could be. There are writers, perhaps great ones, and, certainly, many short story writers who are Catholic. Why isn't there contemporary Catholic fiction? We tried to find a publisher dedicated to Catholic fiction, but we could not find one. We tried to find a Catholic fiction literary prize that might guide us to recent works of Catholic fiction, but we could not find one.

As Catholics and all other Christians know, we live in a world filled with the presence of God—a living God. We have always believed that our stories should reflect this fact, this reality. We believe in redemption, forgiveness, grace, and love—a true love born from God. We may live in a broken world with fallible people, including ourselves, but God's grace enters this reality.

Maybe it was a nudge from above, or simply a human insight that caused us to found and launch Tuscany Press. Certainly, it was, in part, because of our strong belief that the stories we read should reflect the truth of God's presence, a loving presence.

Tuscany Press began in June 2012 and the Tuscany Prize for Catholic Fiction—Short Stories was born. We want to encourage writers of Catholic fiction. We want to publish as many writers of Catholic fiction as possible, and short stories are fun to read.

The doors of Tuscany Press were opened, and before we had a fully operational Web site, we received manuscripts. The short stories started showing up—eventually, many stories. Before we knew it, we had more than a hundred short stories, and they kept coming.

They came from all over the country and outside the United States. The stories came from rural areas, cities, and the suburbs, and from Catholics, Christians of all denominations, and some non-Christians. Authors dusted off old stories from more than twenty years ago, and young writers sent in their stories. We had priests and religious and lay-people sharing with us stories of faith and the presence of God.

After experiencing all these stories, I rediscovered how much fun short stories are to read. In fact, we had so many well-written short stories that we decided to change the 2012 Tuscany Prize for a Catholic Fiction—Short Story collection: We would keep the first-, second-, third-, fourth-, and fifth-place winners, and add five Honorable Mentions.

This Catholic short story collection, we hope and believe, brings God's loving presence to readers in smaller bites, in a format that involves less commitment than, say, a novel, but each story is no less driven by fallible people who, somehow, experience God's grace.

May each of these stories carry the light of redemption, forgiveness, love, and grace, and may each reader discover and bask in this light.

In His Peace and Grace,
Peter J. Mongeau
Publisher
Tuscany Press

Introduction

"She would have been a good woman," The Misfit said,
"if it had been somebody there to shoot her every minute
of her life."

So closes Flannery O'Connor's short story "A Good Man Is Hard to Find." It is the final significant moment of the story and one that points up the moment when the grandmother—and the reader—discovers her ultimate and unseen destiny. It is also one of the more famous examples of what was being written during the heyday of the so-called Catholic Renaissance of postwar America. What's most remarkable about this Catholic literary "moment" is that despite being so brief, it would have a profound impact on future writers, Catholic and non-Catholic alike.

Somewhere in the middle of his memoir *Swimming with Scapulars: The Confessions of Young Catholic,* the Catholic author Matthew Lickona recalls how during his heady young days as a college student he discovered these writers of the Catholic Renaissance—and specifically the late Southern Catholic writer Walker Percy. Years later, Lickona relates that Percy's "words had already sunk deep into me, taking up residence in my long-term memory. They still bubble up in all sorts of situations, little moments of *a-ha* recognition."

Those readers familiar with Catholic fiction in general and Flannery O'Connor's story in particular probably already know about Mr. Lickona's "little moments of *a-ha* recognition." For those readers who have yet to acquaint themselves, those moments depend on the unique perspective on the sacred that Catholic fiction writers bring to their usually secular subject matter.

Here's how Ms. O'Connor explains it in her essay "Novelist and Believer":

"I have to make the reader feel, in his bones if nowhere else, that something is going on here [in a story] that counts," she writes. "Distortion in this case is an instrument; exaggeration has a purpose, and the whole structure of the story or novel has been made what it is because of belief. This is not the kind of distortion that destroys; it is the kind that reveals, or should reveal."

Serving as shorthand for the sorts of startling revelations that, as O'Connor points out, Catholic fiction reveals—or ought to reveal—Mr. Lickona's "*a-ha* recognition" indicates that he, like so many other readers, has hit upon the very earmark of modern Catholic writers.

Of course, that statement begs a number of questions: What makes a writer "Catholic"? What puts the "Catholic" in a novel or short story in the first place? What distinguishes the revelations found in "Catholic" fiction from, say, that of Jewish, Protestant, Muslim, or, for that matter, Hittite fiction?

Getting one's hands around the term "Catholic fiction" or "Catholic novelist" or even "Catholic storyteller" tends to be a slippery affair. Does a Catholic writer acquire his bona fides by throwing some Catholic elements—say, a priest distributing Holy Communion or hearing a dramatic death-bed confession—into his story as a Hollywood director would employ special effects? Does Catholic fiction merely explain or simplify tenets of the faith by rendering the catechism in storybook form? Is a story truly Catholic only if it has a happy ending or an edifying "moral" for both children and adults?

It would be easier to describe the taste of a turnip, the smile on the Mona Lisa's face, or the cut of your house key than to offer a definition of Catholic fiction broad enough to address these questions and encompass all examples or specific enough to account for all writers who are considered "Catholic" in their outlook and approach to fiction writing.

Consider what this task entails. First of all, such a definition must avoid overplaying the term "Catholic fiction." After all, F. Scott Fitzgerald and Ernest Hemingway were Catholics who happened to write (or, perhaps to be more precise, writers who happened to be Catholic)—does that make them automatically Catholic writers? The definition must also avoid inflating the term into a distinction without difference. There is the danger of rendering Catholic fiction a matter of, as James Joyce would describe the Catholic Church in general, "here comes everybody!" For example, do Willa Cather's dying archbishop and the creepy Catholic priests who show up in Stephen King's horror stories automatically place these non-Catholic writers in the same clubhouse as J. F. Powers and Graham Greene, two Catholic writers who cut their men of the cloth from the whole cloth of fiction?

Now, there was a time when distinguishing literature as "Catholic" made as much sense as asking for a cup of "wet water." Count for sure all the great storytellers of Western Civilization since the advent of Christ among those who took their Catholicism in even doses with their tales—Dante, Chaucer, Rabelais, Boccaccio, arguably even Shakespeare, and so forth. All these writers were influenced by and in turn influenced the Catholic milieu that existed before Nietzsche proclaimed God dead and writers started falling over themselves to be the first to write His definitive obituary.

With the highly exaggerated reports of God's demise and other humorous thoughts, we return then to Mr. Lickona's "little moments of *a-ha* recognition." Far from being dead, God is very much alive in the stories presented here. The ultimate agent of grace, God serves as a sort of theater manager in fiction, enhancing the revelations readers find in each story by ensuring that the sound and house lights, as it were, are adjusted to enable the actors to hit their marks as the drama unfolds. Readers are invited to experience this same sort of "a-ha" moment in the short stories presented in Tuscany Press's Collected Short Stories.

The first-place winner of the Tuscany short story prize is Kristin Britten's "Eyes That Pour Forth." Set in a faraway monastery, Britten's story shows—literally—through her character's eyes the miracle and mystery of ordinary life. In "The Reasons Why," the second-place winner, Mollie Ficek touches on another such mystery when she relates the story of Marcy and her aunt Grace, who, suffering from dementia, offers her niece an invaluable lesson in unconditional love and inexplicable human suffering. Human suffering again serves as the psychological setting of third-place-winner Kaye Park Hinckley's "Moon Dance," although in this story Anna, with the help of her husband Will, discovers that forgiveness is a necessary third partner in the dance of love and life.

The fourth-place winner, "True or False," by Bud Scott, sets a familiar scene for Catholic readers, but the confessional box in which Father Timothy and his unnamed "sinner" meet shows us why the doctor is often in as much need of healing as is the patient. Likewise, in fifth-place-winner Michael Piafsky's "Water," desperate housewife Carol finds herself at wits' end in a difficult marriage and hopes to reconnect with her newborn son through three drops of water—and discovers along the way the wellspring of love.

In no particular order, five additional stories are included in the present volume because, judging their quality of merit similar to that of the five winners, the Tuscany editors couldn't let these efforts go unnoticed. "The Debt," by L. C. Ricardo, returns us to the hospital setting as her character Lola comes to understand an important lesson in sin and forgiveness. In Caroline Valencia-Dalisay's "Excess Baggage," forgiveness proves its power by reaching halfway around the globe.

In her short and bittersweet "Morning Star," S. L. Scott does Milton one better by letting God speak for Himself on why and with what great sadness He let the Morning Star fall from the sky as part of His will. A second story of Kaye Park Hinckley's, "Intensive Care," also appears in this volume, and in it she shows that the patient is not always the one in most need of care. Last, Mathew Zimmerer's "Near Miss" invites us to live in the moment and realize that such a moment is God's way of letting us reacquaint ourselves with the miracle of life.

As a working definition, I propose that what distinguishes "Catholic fiction"—and especially the stories contained in these pages—is the unique perspective a writer affords the reader, a perspective informed with what can be called a sacramental view of reality. Avoiding the fruitless abstraction of the idealist and the spiritual bankruptcy of the materialist, the soul thus formed is capable of holding the material world and the spiritual world in one act of imagination. By navigating this narrow way, the Catholic fictionist is telling his reader that the stuff of this world is in a sense as important as the stuff of the next; such a storyteller also offers evidence that clues to the next world can be found hidden in the stuff of this world. In fact, if there's anyone to point to as progenitor of this theory, might we not look to God Himself, molding man like a divine glassblower, blowing his divine spirit into this bit of sand and dust we call flesh to give us our human form and function?

It is perhaps no accident that Catholic writers such as G. K. Chesterton and Graham Greene wrote mystery novels. After all, at the heart of things for Catholics, isn't all of life a mystery, tied intimately and irrevocably to the Pascal Mystery who is Christ? Put this way, we could very well consider the life of faith as one "a-ha!" moment magnified over a lifetime. (In fact, Catholic writers could do worse than take Mary's *"a-ha!"* response to God, "The Magnificat," as a standard in their prayer repertoire.)

Many if not all the stories we received for the Tuscany Short Story Prize demonstrate that this "a-ha" moment is crucial to telling a Catholic story. But as always happens when a large pool of talent accepts an invitation to a party, naming the winners wasn't easy. Nonetheless, after receiving an overwhelming response in the number and quality of submissions, the Tuscany editors judged that the ten stories you now have in your hands deserve to be at the top of the pile.

Our criteria were at once simple and effective—does the story capture the imagination? Is it well written? Does it show the reader more than it tells? Does it, to borrow the novelist John Gardner's idea, maintain the "fictional dream"? In other words, is the story fully and most perfectly crafted to engage the reader's desire to hear a story? Does the story's structure fulfill the basic Aristotelian demand for "a beginning, a middle, and an end"? And finally, does it present characters who will live on long after the story on the page ends?

In the ten stories that make up Tuscany Press's Collected Short Stories—both the five prize winners and the five honorable mentions— I believe these questions are answered with a clear and unequivocal *"A-ha!"*

Editing the Tuscany Press's *Selected Short Stories* was truly a labor of love—with equal emphasis placed on both *labor* and *love*. That said, the work of channeling, corralling, and shaping talents, personalities, ideas, and images was not accomplished single-handedly. First, I thank Tuscany's founder and publisher, Peter Mongeau, for his courage and conviction in deciding to take a chance by investing in Catholic culture—and Catholic fiction in particular. I also thank the writers without whom, obviously, this book would not be possible: Karen Britten, Mollie Ficek, L. C. Ricardo, Kaye Park Hinckley, Bernard Scott, Michael Piafsky, Caroline Valencia-Dalisay, Laura Ricardo, S. L. Scott, and Mathew Zimmerer.

In addition, I thank Father Eric Berns, of the Diocese of La Crosse, Wisconsin, for his wise counsel and welcome advice on sacramental and other spiritual matters related to the stories herein; my brother-in-law Christopher Carstens, director of the Office of Sacred Worship for the Diocese of La Crosse, for his advice on certain liturgical questions; and Arthur and Theresa Hippler, Bernardo Aparicio, Jonathan Potter, Jonathan Webb, Brian Jobe, John Liem, Dorian Speed, and especially Matthew Lickona for their support and guidance. My father, Patrick O'Brien, also gets a word of thanks for the great advice he first gave me back in my high school years—advice I've depended on ever since: "Want to be a good writer? Read!" (The same advice holds, it is hoped, for being a good editor!)

Finally, I'd like to thank my wife, Cecilia, and our eight children, Barbara, Seamus, Bernadette, Norah, Liam, Anastasia, Mara Naomi, and Lucy, for their love and patience throughout this endeavor—and without whom editing Tuscany Press's *Selected Short Stories* would not have been nearly as meaningful.

JOSEPH O'BRIEN
Editor
Tuscany Press

To all writers of Catholic Fiction

May you know God's Beauty, Love, and Peace,
may your work be infused with His Grace,
and may Our Lady watch over you.

Selected Short Stories

Eyes That Pour Forth

Karen Britten

Brother Michael remembers finding the girl standing in the doorway of the Tanzanian monastery where he lives. She is holding the remnants of her eyes in her hands—milky white orbs with pink muscle attached to them like the trails of twin comets. She doesn't cry, but she trembles and quivers in the door frame, and the other monks, white Franciscans from places like Scarsdale, New York, and Wichita, Kansas, gather around her and embrace her with robed arms. They find out that she can see from those eyes when she describes the room in detail: the tanned hide lamp by the oak table, the woodstove by the front door.

After it is established that the fifty-pound girl is a miracle from God, the clotted sockets where her eyes used to be are wrapped several times over in white gauze. Brother Michael learns that it was her mother who took a knife to the girl's face because she kept walking into her mother's room while she worked. Her mother didn't want to see her with all those men, so she grabbed a knife and made it so she couldn't. Only the girl didn't want to stay with her mother after that; she picked up her eyes from the hard-packed-dirt floor and walked to the monastery. She knew to go there because she would often follow her mother and brother there when they needed food or their bodies fixed.

The monks name her Lucy after the saint.

Brother Michael often cries when he sees her, when he looks at those eyes in her hand. She reminds him of the suffering in the world, of mothers giving birth to stillborn boys, men losing legs to accidents in the field, AIDS patients, and malaria infestations. He picks her up after all she's been through and lets her rest her head on his shoulder as he carries her into a vacant room down the hallway. He places her under plaid bedsheets thrown over a wooden plank before dropping her eyes into a plastic cup filled with saline solution.

"Brother," Lucy says. "Will you take me to the ocean?"

"Why do you want to go to the ocean?" he says.

"To see the waves and the sand like I used to."

He sees her smile a baby-toothed grin of ivory.

"You can't go outside," he says. "You can't go anywhere now because people will think you're a witch or something evil."

"But why?"

"Because they don't understand you. They'll take your eyes because they think they'll give them strength."

"But why?"

"Because they fear what they don't understand."

"But *why*?"

"You'll stay with us and be safe."

He watches that smile turn to a frown and then he leaves her because she won't stop tearless-sobbing. She won't stop heaving and moaning and coughing. And though he wants to comfort her, he wants her to stop more than anything, and it will take too long for her to cry herself to sleep.

When he says his prayers that night, he prays for guidance. He's prayed for guidance every night since joining the Order in his twenties, ever since he had a dream of St. Francis holding a bleeding heart in his hands, thorns adorning his bald head. He never again had another dream like it.

Sometimes, Lucy escapes the confines of the monastery while no one is watching, while Brother Michael is praying and eating bread and drinking wine with the others, or tending to the visitors in need of healing. They are so busy with their duties that she simply slips out unnoticed with the other boys and girls who run past aching mothers and their hungry babies.

But she returns to the monastery because she thinks she hears a lion in the grass outside, or because the men stare at her for too long when she walks down the street with gauze over her face and her eyes in her hands, even though she conceals them in the palm of her clasped hand pulled tight into her abdomen, her vision filtered through the light made by the opened slits between the fingers of her right hand. She thinks they look at her like they would a devil; they sometimes point at the gauze and shake their heads. And she runs back to the monastery as fast as she can because the men look like they might approach her, and she remembers what Brother Michael told her about them.

So she decides to stay in the monastery to wander its confines and watch the brothers pray and sing and try to fix people before they die. She watches Brother Michael most of all because she wants to rest her head on his shoulder again, because he moves slowly with her against him and she has never been held like that before. And she watches Father Thomas too, the only man who sews the stitches and catches the babies when they're born, the only man who dresses in black. Only *he* gets to hold up the gold cup when they all go to pray below the bleeding man hanging from the ceiling.

And she does not know—because she is too young and sheltered to know—that the only man who wears black would wear that color anyway, even if he left the priesthood. She doesn't know that Father Thomas is still mourning his failed life, that he once had a wife and wanted a family. Lucy doesn't know his wife didn't want to have children with him because she said he had a cold touch, and she left him to have children with another man. His wife thought he always seemed distant, that when she was crying before him, describing her loneliness and inadequacies to him, he looked at her as he would a wound that needed to be stitched and washed clean. His wife also told him that her new husband ran his hands through her hair when she cried.

Lucy doesn't know that Father Thomas went into the priesthood hoping God would give him warmth in heaven as long as he agreed to follow His rules on earth. That he begged God to give him a family of sorts, like Abraham and his star-children, if he followed the Church's rules. That he determined that eternal bliss meant earthly sacrifice, and that to be content in one life you had to toil in another.

Lucy doesn't know this about Father Thomas, but she sees the lines form on Father Thomas's forehead and his mouth tighten when he's deep in thought; she tries not to laugh, but she isn't able to control it. She thinks his shoulder must be cold and she doesn't like it when he's near her. She finds herself avoiding him because when he moves, he's fast and jumpy and always frowning.

Lucy laughs at the priest's face as he stitches up a boy her age, and Brother Michael looks at her, dropping the gauze in his hands before trying to shoo her away with a flick of his hand. Father Thomas is still unaware that she is observing them when he looks over at her and scowls. The last time he caught her where she shouldn't be, he made her read the Bible as a punishment. Lucy holds her breath and tightens her fingers around her eyes.

In the monastery, after Father Thomas finishes with the groaning people in the main room and retires to his office and closes the door, Lucy follows him and pushes her eyes through the crack under the door to look inside. She wants to know what he does when he's alone, why he spends so many hours locked up in his room. She sees him with his head cradled in his hands, and she thinks she hears him crying because he sounds like the women giving birth or the little boys with broken arms. After a few minutes, he rises to his feet and walks to the door, only she can't get her eyes back because she can't find a way to grab them and pull them under the door. He almost steps on them as he turns the handle, and finds her kneeling on the other side.

"There must be consequences," he says to her as he picks up her eyes with one hand and grabs her by the arm with the other and leads her to her bedroom, where he opens up the dog-eared child's version of the Bible in her native language and places it on her bed. The book is open to the story of Abraham and Isaac. "These are great men who obey. Read it and tell me how Abraham was submissive to God."

When he leaves, she tries to read the story, but her mind starts to wander. She sits back in her chair and crosses her arms until Brother Michael enters the room. Lucy looks up and wants to lean her head against his shoulder again.

"Sing, sing, sing," she sings, the words to a song only she understands.

"You can't go into Father Thomas's room," he says, kneeling on the floor beside her. "He needs privacy, as we all do."

"Why?" she says.

"Some say when you're alone, you're closest to God."

"I don't like being alone," she says.

"Maybe when you're older you will."

"But I just want to go outside and play."

"I know you do, but I can't always take you outside to play. I can't always watch you."

"I want to go now."

"I have to pray. Not tonight."

"You're always praying."

He sighs and looks at the opened book. Then he gets up, takes the Bible in his hands, and tosses it to the floor, where the dust lives eternally among the boards. "You just need to know for now that Jesus Christ was a good man because he played with the animals and talked to God and had love for all things," he says.

Only she is more occupied with a scab on her hand from the last time she did cartwheels in the thickets, and she picks at it while Brother Michael speaks.

"Lucy," he says, "when you sleep, do you see everything in the room since you can't close your eyes?"

"Oh no," she says. "No, Brother, when I sleep my eyes have fun and fly to a place where boys talk to goats and ride purple horses in fields of blue grass and white water. And it's always light there—it's never dark—and no one seems to notice me, but my eyes see everything."

"Do you want to stay there or would you rather be here?"

"I want to stay there, but I wake up because all living things wake up at some point."

He smiles while she stands on the bed with her arms opened for him to hold her, but he tells her he needs to leave because he has to pray, so she jumps up and down and makes a whiny noise from her throat that gets louder when her feet hit the bed. He asks her to stop but she doesn't; he raises his voice and tells her to stop. He purses his lips. She does as he asks. She sits back down on the bed and crosses her arms.

"I'm sorry," he says. "But you have to be quiet."

"You said you'd take me to the water."

He walks to the door.

"It isn't safe for you to be out there," he says.

He closes the door, but she wants to leave. She wants to explore the rooms of the monastery and see what the monks do in their rooms alone, to see if they cry like Father Thomas. But she wants to leave the monastery as well, to explore the world beyond the walls as she used to with her mother and brother. She wants to go the ocean and pick up the sand with her hands and feel the water surround her feet. She wants to run and feel her heart beat fast. She wants to see things, Brother Michael decides, but not the things that make her leave her mother and join a monastery; not the things that make her put down her blindness—the things that make her want to pick up her sight and light out into the world.

Brother Michael wants to see things too, but he hasn't been able to see much lately. He hasn't been able to see the importance of his vocation in years. Rituals that he once took solace in are now redundant and he doesn't know how to deal with complacency. He joined the Franciscans and said good-bye to his single mother in Brooklyn because he felt a great love for the sacrifice and service of the Lord, but now all he feels is the implacable stare of the wooden man hanging from the wooden cross. Realizing he may not have come to the monastery to see, as Lucy sees, he came because he wanted to turn away—he always wants to turn away.

Brother Michael takes her outside the next day and he holds her eyes as she does frog-leaps and somersaults on the grounds behind the building, where walls of grass create a barrier between the monastery and the rest of the wild world. He positions his hands so that she can see herself and she occasionally walks up to him and moves his hands to get a better view of herself.

"Hold them higher!" she yells in the middle of a flip.

He holds them higher.

Watching her play, he wonders what's best for her. He sees her wipe small hairs from her sweaty forehead and smile. She doesn't do much smiling, only when she's outside or when someone makes a funny face. He wonders if she should be somewhere beyond the grass, whether she would even survive on her own. He wonders if living in a monastery for the rest of her life would even work, or if at some point they would have to let her leave to battle the unforgiving land around her. Could he send her on a plane for the first time to some part of the United States? He doesn't think it would even matter. The people there would not be any more tolerant than people here. He wonders if he could convince her to live in community for the rest of her life like a relic in the corner, with lights around her and worshippers who come to greet her with their afflictions, seeking her guidance, her healing powers, or her prayers.

And then he curses God for this miracle of His. He tells God that He is cruel for letting this happen to her and allowing her to be this way. He feels the heat of finitude in his gut when he realizes she might die for this gift of His if they set her free, but then he remembers that she should have died from the knife, and that she was saved for some reason. He wishes he knew what that reason was. He wants it all to make sense.

When she finishes playing, she grabs her eyes and walks back inside. He tells her to go to her room and she submits, closing the door behind her. He knows that it won't be long before she leaves her room again to wander the monastery with her eyes in her hand.

That night Lucy makes her way to the chapel and sees Father Thomas praying inside. His hands are clasped so that she can see the white of his knuckles. His head is peering down toward the wood floors with dust and the Holy Spirit between the crevices. She walks closer to him, trying not to make the boards creak, but the chapel is always still and she can't keep silent.

"Come here and kneel next to me," he says to her.

She kneels on the floor. It hurts her knees, but she knows the monks like to feel that way sometimes. It brings them closer to the world of suffering, to the wounds of Jesus, they say. At least that's what she remembers them saying. She places her eyes in the pew, and they watch Father Thomas.

"What are you doing?" she asks as he bows his head and closes his eyes.

"Praying. Have you prayed tonight?"

She says she hasn't.

"You must pray every night," he says. "How do you pray?"

"With my hands together like this."

She mimics his grasp and leans her head back.

"What do you pray for?"

"For all the brothers; for all the men," she says.

"That's good. You need to pray for all of us to be good men who live by the law of God. When God permits us to be without something, we are to pray for happiness with His decision, to be grateful for what God has given us."

"What has God given us?" she asks.

"Life, love, friendship. A roof over our heads and food to eat. What are you grateful for?"

"I don't know," she says.

"You need to pray harder then," he says.

He takes Lucy's hands and clasps them with his own. He squeezes them together so she cannot pull hers away even if she wants to.

"This is how you'll do it, Lucy. Like this."

She tries to endure the pain, but it feels as if the bones in her hands might break, so she makes a moaning sound like a cat before a fight and he stops squeezing. She presses her hands together as he told her to, so that they start shaking and her knuckles turn white. She stops because she doesn't like how it feels and grabs her eyes instead, scanning the room with them. She is distracted by something on the altar, so she jumps to her feet and walks toward it.

"Did you know that I always wanted a child?" he asks, watching her stand underneath Christ's feet.

But Lucy's attention is elsewhere and she doesn't respond. Instead, she stares at the beaten Christ with a crown of thorns on his head and painted blood running down his face. She walks up to the altar and grabs the chair Brother Michael sits on during Mass, and she stands on it because she thinks the blood is real and wants to see if it's real.

"Child, come back," he says, the lines forming again on his forehead.

She stands on the chair and stretches her body and her arm as long as it will go, and she reaches with a finger to touch the blood of Christ. It's warm, wet, and thick, like wet paint in the afternoon sun. It stays on her finger when she pulls her hand away and she places it on her tongue. The taste makes her face scrunch up and she swallows it to get the taste out of her mouth.

Father Thomas grabs her from the chair and places her on the ground next to him. When Brother Michael walks in, Father Thomas's right hand is wrapped over the girl's shoulder, and he is wiping the blood from her finger with the other one. Brother Michael can see the red from the chapel's entrance, so he runs down the aisle toward them.

"Is she okay?" Brother Michael asks.

"Someone must have repainted the blood on the statue," Father Thomas says.

"Nobody painted it," Brother Michael responds, knowing that any maintenance in the chapel would have had to come through his office.

"Then she cut her hand," Father Thomas said.

Father Thomas finishes wiping the girl's finger, inspects it, and finds no cut.

"I'm going to go see who did this," he says.

He leaves.

But Father Thomas doesn't return to the chapel, because he can't find anyone who admits to painting the head of Christ, and as Brother Michael waits in vain, letting Lucy rest on his shoulder, he makes up his mind about the girl. As he hears the rain begin to fall against the monastery's roof, he thinks he can see the blood of Christ dripping down the statue's face from the crown on his head.

"Lucy, I'd like to take you to the ocean," he says.

"You'll take me now?" she asks. "But it's dark."

"That's the best time to see the ocean, when the moon is out and it hovers over the water."

Together they walk out of the chapel.

It's humid outside, but the evening rain has stopped, leaving behind a continuous dripping of remnant water from the billowing trees above the building. It drops on Brother Michael's face, but he doesn't mind. He relishes the feeling of cool water in the humidity and mist of the hot night.

He loads her into the only car on the premises, a ten-year-old jeep, and hopes that the engine doesn't wake anyone, but it won't matter anyway. Even if it did wake the whole monastery, they would already be gone by the time the monks found out, so he doesn't care that it sputters when he turns the key.

He drives through town, past the men still chatting over sodas and beers, their shirts wet and their faces dewy even though none of them seems to notice or care. He drives past trees with leaves bigger than Lucy's head, past cows and their enemies lurking in the grass, past barking dogs and trash fires.

And when he sees the ocean, he starts crying. Tears form and he lets them fall onto his cheeks and lips and down his chest, where his heart beats quickly in the dark distance of this place. He parks the car where the road stops and he grabs her hand, walking with her toward the water of a remote part of the coast that the fishers leave alone because it's too open; the waves are too high and the fish like the coves so much better.

Lucy hands him her eyes and runs into the water, then she falls to her knees and lets the water collapse over her body. She laughs, and he thinks it sounds like a bird's whistle in the sea breeze. He watches her run out of the water and onto the rocky sand, unbeaten by the waves. She trips and falls to her knees several times, but each time she gets up, laughing. She changes her mind and doesn't like the sand anymore, so she swims instead.

Brother Michael reminds himself that Saint Lucy would've rather died than submit to human forces around her. She was saved from death by God only to be given eternal life. She went blind to see the face of God, the face of the Son, and she held those eyes out for the rest to see because they were not what mattered most; they were merely a veil before the true vision that bled from within. And because of her unwillingness to cave in to the world, she was granted immortality. Brother Michael wants nothing less for the young girl playing on the beach before him now. He wants to lose Lucy so she could be found, leave her so that she might find greater union with God and all His things. He realizes she might die, but he accepts death so that she might find life, because to him, there's nothing worse than stagnancy, than being kept inside like a wooden relic.

"Higher!" Lucy yells to him.

He holds her eyes higher.

But after almost an hour of her delight, he calls the girl over and tells her to take her eyes from his hands.

"But I want to see me play," she says.

"I want you to take your eyes, and I want you to explore. The coast is longer than you think it is, longer than what you see here. I want you to walk alone for a while."

"Are there men here?"

"There might be. Don't talk to them. Keep walking. They will think you're not real, a figment of their imagination. Do you know what that means?"

"No," she says.

"It means they won't believe in you, and that will be fine because they'll keep moving on with their lives. You will be free to wander."

Her face is still and her eyes are fixated on his. She lifts them higher and then turns them side to side as if scanning his face. He swallows and wipes the dew from his forehead, but he lets the water pour from his eyes.

"Go with me," she says.

"I'm not allowed, but I'll be right here when you come back."

She doesn't look like she believes him; at least that's what he thinks. He thinks she can read his mind and know his intentions, the true vision behind the veil. But she complies and leaves him anyway, turning toward the ocean in a cadence of feet thumping against hard sand. Brother Michael feels her presence in the salty breeze and foamy air that wash up on his face.

He watches her walk along the water's edge, away from sight. The moon glistens over the water, causing lines of white to form over the incessant motion of the waves and the life that teems below them. He waits a few minutes and watches the space where he last saw her before walking toward the jeep and getting inside. He holds the car key in his hand, letting it dangle from its chain and sparkle in the moonlight. While his heart is heavy, he looks outside one more time through the window and thinks he sees her standing before him, but it's only the ghost of her: the outline of a shadow with two white eyes held high in her hands.

The Reasons Why

Mollie Ficek

I was seven years old the first time my mother left. My father, in his pickup truck, and me along beside him in my purple pajama gown, drove to where she ran. We brought her home in just three days.

The first time, she left a letter, a small thing, the nearly transparent paper folded in half and written in her careful hand. It lay on the dashboard on the way to find her, and all the way home, too, as she sat next to my father and looked out the window. I watched her face in profile from the backseat and the hair that fell in front of it. Sunlight threw glare across the dirty windshield and lit her hair like it was on fire, so that years later I would remember it red.

My father and I were triumphant from our trip for too long, and soon she was gone again. The second time my mother left, she didn't leave a thing.

Overnight the weather changed. Leaves flutter on their branches, and that nostalgic smell of autumn—earth and wind and something else strong and nameless—blows through my open window. Nothing smells like the smell of fall. I light a cigarette and steer my car through Friday traffic on my way to pick up Grace.

Grace spends Monday through Friday on the other side of town in an adult daycare center called Four Winds, for those with memory loss and dementia. The building is cream stucco. On my way inside, whenever I visit, I have made a habit of dragging my hand across the exterior wall. I let the crags and notches in the concrete scratch away the negative energy of work and my wandering mind so that I can always enter with a smile. Grace deserves a smile. And so do the rotating hourly staff of nursing assistants and receptionists and bed makers and bath givers and dietary aides, those who do the job I can no longer do Monday through Friday.

Inside it is warm. The air smells of laundry and solvents and alcohol wipes and the elderly. I greet Jenna at the desk.

"Good day?" I ask.

"Always is around here," she says, with an eyebrow lifted to the sky and a worn smile that reads *Praise His holy name for it.*

I appreciate her belief in a higher power—it helps her give kindness and attention to those the world is weary with. My job does not promote kindness. My job makes me answer phones, and take appointments, and restock coffee tables with magazines, and hand out toothbrushes and floss to patients when their cheeks are swollen after teeth cleanings. It makes me waste hours counting minutes. It makes me multiply those minutes by individual dollars and pray to make it out ahead. It makes my stomach turn at the end of each month when the bills take over my living room floor. It makes me frown every day until the stucco walls of every evening force a smile on my face.

I find Grace at the dining room table with a puzzle spread out in front of her, the image of a pony in wildflowers taking shape within the scattered pieces. I squeeze her shoulders the way I always do and kiss the top of her head where her hair is thin.

Grace no longer speaks. I've read all the literature. I know what that means. But she knows me still. I can tell by the way she takes my arm when she's scared, and the way she nods at me or squeezes my hand when I ask her questions, and the way her eyes look, like they've always looked at me. Like I belong to her. Like she's going to take care of me.

I am helping Grace fit pieces in place when I see Stephanie come out of the kitchen. Stephanie has beautiful brown hair with a wave and a wide smile with white teeth. All the male residents flirt with her, which she takes, always, in good humor. Last week, she told me she was pregnant, nine weeks already, and I cried on the drive home because of it. She'll leave in a few months on maternity and we won't see her anymore. Stephanie's the apple of my Grace's eye, sneaks her extra cookies after dinner, and besides that, she's a damn good nurse.

"I was wondering if you'd be working today," I say.

"It's been a wild one."

"That's what Jenna said."

"Did she tell you about our new permanent resident?"

"What do you mean 'permanent'?" I say.

I look at Grace, who is studying a green puzzle piece.

Stephanie whispers, "They call it 'granny dumping.'"

I laugh out loud. I can't help myself.

"Shh!" she says, and giggles. She prepares a Dixie cup of pills from one of the locked cupboards.

"It doesn't mean what you think."

"Granny dumping?" I am whispering, too.

"Someone dropped her off this morning."

Stephanie nods toward an old woman in a recliner. The woman sleeps with her mouth open, a black hole. She doesn't have teeth and doesn't wear dentures. I can see where her lips sink in around the walls of her gums.

"When Tiff got here this morning, she was in the parking lot with a sign around her neck. It said, MY NAME IS DORIS. There was a letter, too. Said she didn't have anywhere to live or anyone to take care of her anymore."

"People actually do that?" I ask, horrified, imagining Grace alone, in an early-morning parking lot with a sign around her small neck. Then I picture Doris's daughter, wiping tears as she drives away into the dark wide open morning.

"People do it. She's sleeping proof," Stephanie says, gesturing to the napping old woman.

"Where will she go?"

"The paperwork's already moving for her to go to the nursing home on Division. It happens more than you think. And in this economy."

I swallow hard.

"It happens here?"

"A couple of times. None in a while. More often they're left at hospitals or police stations, like women do with babies."

I look again at the woman in the recliner.

"That's terrible," I say.

"That's life. Or the end of it, anyway."

The second time my mother left, my stomach ached to go after her. It wasn't really that I wanted her back, or even that I knew what it would feel like when she was gone for good. Instead, I wanted that time on the road with my father, the sunshine and the fall weather and the miles and miles behind us. I wanted the freedom of skipping school and I wanted to smell the trees as they passed and feel the air gritty and fast against my open hand.

But the second time she left, we had no grand adventure. My father buckled me into the backseat of his pickup truck, pinched between the cab and a suitcase, of all my things. He didn't play his music for me, the rock and roll booming from the dashboard. He didn't buy me licorice and bubblegum and chocolate bars and spits. He didn't talk to me like a grown-up, or tell me things about my mother or his life before her, or about me when I was a baby and he was a brand-new dad.

Instead he drove fast and with a hard jaw. He drove all the way to the Badlands and left me on a farm down a long gravel road that belonged to my great aunt Grace.

At home, I sit Grace in front of the old television and pop a videotape into the VHS player. She likes to watch an episode of *Murder, She Wrote* at seven o'clock and then another before she goes to bed. By now,

I've seen them all—each tape rewound a hundred times. Every mystery solved. Every chapter tapped out on the keys of that woman's typewriter.

I mix tuna fish with ranch dressing and eat it out of the can. Grace has already eaten, for which I am thankful. The cupboards are deep and they are empty.

Two weeks ago, I saw a lawyer on my lunch break. I brought a double-bagged grocery sack full of bills and receipts and bank statements. I set it on his desk like I was delivering lunch.

We have a lot of options, he said. *Don't worry.*

By the end of our meeting, after the bag was upturned and the calculations made, the options were boiled down to two.

Chapter 7 or *Chapter 13?*

Grace likes to hold my hand while she watches her show. Her small hands are transparent, the veins lifted like smoky blue mountains underneath the mist of her skin. I look at my own. They don't look like hers. I have always wondered whose they look like.

"Ooh, this is a good one," I say. "A boating accident."

Grace looks at me with a worried brow.

"Don't worry," I say. "I won't spill the beans."

She lets go of my hand and pulls her palm across the texture of the couch as if collecting dog hair or pills in the fabric. She hurries herself next, dusting the coffee table. She gets up from the couch and goes to her room. I don't follow but know she's in there, like every night, taking clothes out of drawers and folding them, one by one, on her bed.

Grace had no children of her own, and no husband alive on the earth when I met her. The year after he passed and years before my father brought me to her, she had what the medical community calls a "pelvic exoneration," which means they hollowed her out, took everything south of her navel and made room. Grace wore two bags, one on each hip, that did the work her bladder used to and what was left of her colon. She didn't let this slow her down. She didn't let it harden her.

When I was a girl, Grace taught me how to clean those bags—to empty them in the toilet and run them through with hot water. She taught me how to help her around the house with laundry and dishes and dusting. She taught me how to move hogs before sunup using only my voice and, occasionally, a stock prod. She taught me how to wean baby pigs from their mothers and how to slice off their testicles with razor blades. She taught me how to work hard. And she taught me to be kind, to be respectful. To call men "sir" and women "ma'am."

Grace taught me about Jesus Christ and God and the Holy Ghost, and the Virgin Mother, too. She didn't anger when I lifted my eyebrows and asked questions instead of offering prayers. She didn't talk about my father or my mother, but she didn't stop me from talking about them either. Grace taught me to take care of myself, to take care of my own. She taught me to be thankful for the things I had, even when I didn't have them.

I help Grace dress for bed in a long nightgown, worn almost through. Once she's under the covers, I lie beside her and hold her hand and we look at the ceiling. There we pray together—the same each night.

Hail Mary, full of grace. The Lord is with thee. Blessed art thou among women, and blessed is the fruit of thy womb, Jesus.

I was fourteen, an awkward, lonely thing, living with Grace in the country when her cancer came back, this time resurfacing in her breasts. I was young. I thought, what will *I* do if she dies this time? Where will *I* go?

But Grace didn't die. Instead, she let them cut off her breasts. She let the chemo take care of the rest. *I think God is hell-bent on making me a man,* she said while chewing ice chips in her hospital bed. *I shouldn't have worked so hard like one. I should have baked more.* When her hair grew back, it was different. Not like the dark brown curls she rolled up in a trucker hat when I was little. It grew back lighter, thinner, like she was someone else altogether.

Not long after, we moved to town. Grace sold the farm to pay for the mastectomy. She used what was left of her savings for the chemo.

After Grace is in bed, I spread the bills around me on the floor. I already know the numbers, but I pen them on lined paper and scratch them out anyway. $257 plus $118 plus $54.32 plus $52.30 plus $296 plus $313 plus $786. MasterCard plus Discover plus electricity plus gas plus St. Michael's Health Services plus Visa plus first and second mortgages. Plus $1,800 flat for Grace's care, this month like every other. The dollars pile up and up. I reread the small text and due dates, some already passed. I do this every night as if somehow the numbers could change and even out, as if it was possible I miscounted, miscalculated this whole time, as if all of this could be over and Grace and I could live in peace and small comforts—a new nightgown, fresh episodes of her favorite show.

I light a cigarette. I let the ashes fall onto the paper next to me. I imagine the whole of it going up in flames with me in the middle. I close my eyes and picture the fire consuming me, the house, my dead-beat car, the block, then leaping across town to the bank and to the lawyers and destroying all the paper there, too. When I open my eyes, I see the back door is open. I hadn't heard anything.

By the time I get outside, Grace is halfway over the fence. She has propped up a weathered wicker chair against it and climbed. One leg is almost over.

"Grace! Please don't do that. Don't do that, please!"

I rush to her, and stand below, deciding my next move, trying to calculate hers. She swats her hand at me.

"Grace, please come down from there," I say.

I touch her back and try to pull her leg down from midair. She grunts at me. Her head and chest and one of her feet are above the fence, like a sideways split. I can't help but laugh about what it must look like on the other side.

"Grace," I say with a laugh, and then plead, "Come down!"

The night is chill and quiet. Above us, leaves shake slowly on branches, still green from the attention of summer. Grace tries again to pull herself over, but can't figure where to move her other foot. I hold on to it.

"Sweetheart, come down."

Grace spins her face around and looks at me wild, as if, were she not otherwise occupied, she would hit me square in the face. She tries again to hoist herself over, and her urostomy bag pinches between the fence and her stomach and opens, sending a deluge of urine down her side and onto my arm still holding tight to her foot. Grace doesn't seem to notice. I'm afraid the same will happen to her other bag, and that I'll have to clean that too, so I change my voice.

"Look what you've done." I say it loud. I make it sound strange.

She turns toward me, then back to her business.

"What are you doing? The hogs are loose—they ate through the fence again," I say. "Grace, did you hear me? The hogs are out. I can't get them back in without you."

Grace turns to look at me again. I strip any comfort from my voice.

"Well, are you going to help me or not? I don't know what you're doing that's more important."

Grace searches my face. She's confused, and it kills me, but she relaxes her shoulders.

"Let's move."

She lessens her grip on the fence and begins to get down. I can see the fight has faded, the wild in her eyes wiped away by water.

"Can I help you?"

She nods.

"Come on," I say, softer now. "We'll get them back into the pen by morning."

I put my arm around her and guide her back inside, wash her in the bathroom, and then lead her down the hallway back to bed.

I hated the city. I missed the farm, and the open spaces, where I understood the quiet and wasn't afraid of it, where I enjoyed the easy distractions of nature. I missed the pigs, even if they stank, even if they forced me up at five in the morning to feed them. I missed the way the floor creaked so anywhere in the house I could tell where Grace was. I missed the section lines plump with plums, that bruise of a fruit that tasted better than candy, and the chokecherry bushes overflowing in red, their berries waiting to be turned into jam. I missed the line of photographs that climbed the wall of the staircase and the one at the top, taken by a neighbor, that Grace had sent out as a Christmas card the year after I came to stay—she driving the tractor, me standing tall in the scoop. It was lost, somehow, in the move.

I missed it all. And so did Grace, even as she pretended to have the highest spirits. In town, I felt smothered, watched. In town, I felt Grace's spirits sag, and watched as her skin did the same.

I struggled in high school. I was no good at English or history or making friends. When I was done, I was done. That's what I told Grace. And even though she argued, I could see the weight lift from her shoulders. She quit her second job when I began working at the dentist's office after graduation. I've been there almost ten years now.

When I hear Grace stirring, I wake myself up. On Saturday mornings and on Sundays too, I perform Mass. Long ago we streamlined the parts Grace liked about the process—confession, and communion. After that, we celebrated the abridged ceremony on both weekend days, because they blurred together anyway, and because it was something Grace remembered, something she liked to do.

I move to the kitchen where I tear off a couple of chunks of stale French bread and put them in the microwave. I pour a glass of grape juice from the fridge. I bring these meager offerings to her bedroom. There, Grace busily cleans the closet in her nightgown.

"Time for prayer," I say.

She smoothes her hair, then kneels beside the bed with little trouble. It amazes me how much her musculature remembers—how her body knows to kneel in prayer even as her mind forgets why.

I bring her rosary to her. She counts each bead, worn by her own fingertips, one by one in a circle.

I say the prayers aloud as she counts. My memory works—while I say the Our Father's and the Glory Be's and Mysteries—I think of other things. I think about the cruel beast that is the memory, and how I could tell Grace anything now and she couldn't deny it. I could tell her that she was sweet, but that she barely knew me, that I was the day nurse and another would be by in the evening. Or I could tell her that she was my mother, after all. That her insides weren't abstracted, but that for nine months, they grew me, and that I came out looking like my father. I could tell her that we were never farmers, or that we were but we didn't have to leave, and that she never worked as a cleaning maid and that we were never too poor to send me to college. I could tell her we weren't going to lose this house and this junky car like she hadn't lost her ovaries and her bladder and her breasts. That we could travel, if we wanted, or buy ourselves something nice. I could tell her that I was going to medical school in the fall and that I had met a nice man and remind her that she had met one, too. And I could tell her that when she couldn't remember, it wasn't because she was sick and it wasn't because the folds in her brain were shrinking or expanding or that the synapses were tangling, but that the world itself fluctuated sometimes and that it would be over soon, and that she would remember it all just like I said.

When I am done with my words and Grace with her beads, she bows her head to confess. She knows I am no priest. She knows I cannot absolve her. But long before she lost her voice, she whispered anyway so I couldn't hear her. Grace and I linger there, suspended in the moment of her confession, and I use the quiet to offer my own. I don't speak it aloud. I don't want Grace to hear this. But I let the words part my lips to see how they feel there—*It would be easier to leave you than to do all of this.* After I say it, I know it isn't true. When Grace raises her head, I offer the bread and wine and she takes it, crossing herself. She chews the bread slowly, wetting it to mush inside her mouth with the grape juice wine.

Later, I throw my hair up in a ponytail, then comb through Grace's. I put on my uniform for job number two: black pants, a black tuxedo shirt with the white clip-on bow tie and my name tag that reads MARCY. WELCOME TO REEL DEAL CINEMAS.

I drive Grace across town to Four Winds. It is Saturday. They have different staff on the weekends and I don't know them well. The weekend staff rotates out more quickly—queasy high school students, or the occasional college nursing major with a too-busy schedule, or other people who think they can handle the job, only to find out they can't. This regular turnover must be how these places work, I think, so the weekend staff at the nursing homes I visited back before I found Four Winds wouldn't know Grace. They wouldn't remember me.

I help her get settled in front of the television, where a few residents are watching old TV shows.

"Hi, Agnes, sweetheart," I say and wave. She is flirtatious with the television, and chuckles at an on-screen joke. She has been here for years.

I continue through the room.

"Hi, Bob," I say. I pat his shoulder. He's only six weeks in. This old rerun is still some kind of a thrill.

They both look at me lazily. Grace is agitated. She stands up, and tries to follow me out the door.

"I'll only be a few hours," I say. "Picking up a short shift. I'll be back before you know it."

One of the new nursing assistants helps me resettle Grace into a big recliner. She looks like a child inside it. I scan the room for the woman who was left in the parking lot on Friday morning but can't find her anywhere. She must be moved already into some other place that new people will tell her is home.

Back in my car, I light a cigarette and smoke it down. I let it cartwheel out my open window. I drive on Division and pass the movie theater. I keep going. I drive all the way to the edge of town, where a small park is surrounded by bushy evergreens. I sit on the empty swing set, my butt squeezed between the twinned and taut metal chains and buoyed by the rubber seat of the swing. I light another cigarette.

I lost my second job at the movie theater four weeks ago to a girl named Jessica who was in the tenth grade. They were downsizing. They were sorry. I thought: Who isn't? That first Saturday, I got ready and dropped off Grace like usual and was in the parking lot adjusting my bow tie before I remembered. The second Saturday, I had errands to run and I thought it a perfect excuse, a good time to get a few things done for the week. The third Saturday, I took myself to a coffee shop and slowly sipped a cup of cappuccino that cost $4.95. It had a foamy design on the top, like a leaf or a star. I closed my eyes and relaxed my shoulders and stayed there, sipping the same cold coffee for hours, all by myself. I watched the patrons, watched the dates and the singles, watched teachers grade papers and students write them. I watched a mother come in with her teenage daughters and buy them anything they wanted—extra large coffees and rice-crispy bars the size of my hand.

As I watch my feet dangle from the swing, I stub out my cigarette in the sand, then put the butt back in my pocket. I kick my feet onto the ground and swing. I kick again, swing higher. I pump my legs, out then back and out again, until I'm high on the swing, the wind moving quickly over me, my vantage point climbing higher and higher. I close my eyes and fall back, still holding tight to the chains. I soar above the ground and open my eyes to the sky above my face, in motion. I feel dizzy. I feel that I have been shaken loose, that I am moving now, in some direction, any direction. I feel weightless. I feel free.

When I was twenty-one years old, I left Grace. I didn't know where I was going and I didn't get far. I put twenty dollars of gas in her car and when ten dollars was gone, I turned back around. Grace didn't ask me why I ran away, or why I came back either. I was furious with her for not asking, for not expecting me or encouraging me to explain myself. I wanted so badly for her to accuse so I could spit every sharpened thought that I had been building and bottling for the last thirteen years, every mean thing I could think to say to her.

But Grace held her tongue and, somehow, so did I. And I came to realize, slowly, over the course of that rough year when her back hurt too much to continue working and her memory started slipping enough for me to notice, that it wasn't Grace I wanted to hurt. So I burned it up, that irritation, or I snuffed it out. I got a second job, then after another round of tests for Grace, and no more cancer, I got a second mortgage on the house too.

The first thing Grace forgot was how to wear her bra. She had worn one religiously after the mastectomy, even as the small cups puffed out and held nothing. She wore it to cover the scar that crossed her chest. Grace snapped the clasps around her back each morning before lifting her cleaning rags and sprays and solvents into the trunk of her car. Soon, she had no memory for the movements, how to link the two sides behind her, and she would struggle, confused, in the morning, before setting the bra aside. That one was easy to ignore.

The second thing Grace forgot was my mother. I asked her to retell the story my father told about when they first met—how my mother turned him down at a small-town Fourth of July dance and the refusal lost him five dollars in a bet with his best friend. I asked sometimes, even then, in my early twenties to hear Grace's version of the story, because even though she heard it secondhand, and even though I knew it by heart, she told it differently every time. Sometimes my mother wore a red dress. Sometimes it was black. Sometimes her eyes were soft and gray like mine. Sometimes they were done up in bright makeup like a movie star. I asked Grace to tell me while we waited at her oncologist's office to hear more results.

What do you mean, your mother? she said. *What mother?* I let that hurt me. I let it punch me in the gut like I would never do now, not with anything she said, even if she could say it. But back then, I let it make me angry. I didn't know then that she said things, not intending to hurt, just trying to remember. *Where do you think I came from?* I said, maliciously. *What, do you think I'm yours?* Grace didn't have an answer.

I stay on the swings until the sun has set, and it's too cold to stay longer. When I return to Four Winds, Grace has nodded off with her head at an odd angle in the big recliner as the TV plays *The Lawrence Welk Show*. Lawrence and his guests dance and sing across the stage.

Grace looks just like abandoned Doris sleeping in that chair, except she still has her teeth. I think about Grace in the parking lot with a sign around her neck and a short, simple letter. I think about waiting nearby in the car, watching just to be sure someone finds her.

At home I help Grace get ready for bed. We change her out of her clothes and into her nightgown. She is groggy, goes easily. I know she'll probably wake up again in a few hours, but right now she wants sleep and I don't argue. I want sleep myself. I help her under the covers, then tuck her in. I shut off the light, and lie on the bed next to her, hold her hand and pray.

Holy Mary, Mother of God, pray for us sinners, now and at the hour of our death. Amen.

That night I have a dream, or maybe it's a memory or maybe something else altogether. A thought cloudy with sleep and fluxing between awake and something other. It makes me wake with a question. I wonder: If Grace knew, if she were here as an observer—in her favorite coveralls with her beautiful, long, thick brown hair tumbling out of a trucker hat—instead of the observed, instead of the woman with thin hair in the recliner, would she tell me to go? Would she tell me to do what I had to do?

Grace could be hard sometimes, and strong. When I was nine years old, she made me watch as she set her own finger after she broke it against a rotted door. She made me promise not to look away, but to learn and to listen. *Don't make me say it twice*, she said the first time I cringed and closed my eyes. She didn't have to.

Grace could be soft sometimes too, and kind. In that same year, she hid with me under the covers during a thunderstorm that shook the old farmhouse and lit up the bedroom, even under the quilts, so that it played above us through the colorful patchwork like a twisted kaleido-scope. *It's a gift,* she said. *A show God put on for us.* I didn't believe her, but I loved her there in that moment for holding me, and for shielding me from my fears and the sound of the thunder.

When I wake up, I don't prepare the bread or the fake wine. Instead, I pack a few of Grace's things while she's still asleep—her warmest sweater, her favorite socks, a picture from the dresser of her and her husband on their wedding day.

When Grace wakes, I hurry her together, comb her hair quickly. I beg her to eat some eggs and drink a bit of milk and she looks at me confusedly, like I've forgotten something. Somewhere, she's remember-ing our Mass, just not quite remembering enough. There'll be no con-fession today, no Rosary, no grape juice, no absolution.

I help Grace into the passenger seat of my car and put her suitcase in the backseat. We set out on the road, the sun shining down on us, hazy then bright, already warming the spirited fall day. The road is open. It welcomes us.

Beside me, Grace stares out the window as we leave the city and the fields open up on either side. She watches combines cut down crops. She watches as we speed by farmsteads. She watches tall stalks of corn and sunflowers sway lazily on wide acres. She puts her hand up to the window and follows along all these images, as if she could remember just how it would feel to touch them again.

We drive for hours on highways before they turn to gravel.

I never read my mother's letter. Never read the thin transparent paper that sat on the dashboard for our whole trip. I used to regret that. That used to be my biggest regret. I had all the time, all the possibility, even though I was young and the curiosity wasn't deep because there was no question that she would return. No question that she would stay.

I was envious of her, for years, my mother. After I was angry, I was envious. She got to leave. She got to turn away from responsibility, a husband, a child, and leave without one more word on the matter. I imagined her, when I was young, and then again when I was too old for such fantasies, in some other faraway place, smoking long cigarettes and sipping slow coffee. I imagined her beautiful and carefree and always smiling and always laughing and always with a twinkle in her bright gray eyes.

I'm glad now that I never read it. It's an unopened question from the part of me that's past, just like she is. Just like the reasons why she came back and left again are unopened and the reasons my father did the same, and the reasons why Grace got cancer, and the reasons why she got it again. And the reasons why some people are rich and some people are poor and some people are free and some people are burdened. Or some people are healthy and some people are sick, or why some people remember and some people forget. None of these questions matters. None of them needs opening.

I pull into a long gravel drive. I look at Grace and wonder whether she remembers the way the rocks feel underneath the car, the way they sound, pinging up against the bottom.

We pull past the farmhouse and I park the car. I keep my eyes on Grace. I open the backseat and retrieve her sweater, then help her out of the car and wrap it around her.

"We're home, Grace," I say.

I lead her past the house where she used to live, where she raised me. There's a light on in the living room. I can see a shadow move in front of it. I walk Grace toward the barns. They look different, some even missing, but she doesn't seem to notice. I keep watching her eyes for some kind of recognition.

"Remember here?" I say, and point to the water pump. "We used to haul those buckets full of water two at a time for feeding in the barns. Remember? And you told me that one time, your cousin from Chicago backed into the pump because he couldn't drive the loader and you didn't have water from this well for a week. Do you remember, Grace?"

She reaches out to touch it. We keep walking.

"Remember here?" I say, "where the nursery was? We'd come here first in the morning and feed the sick babies with bottles. We held them like footballs and they suckled down the formula."

Grace smiles, but I know we're not there yet.

"Remember their tails, so long and curly before we cut them?"

"Or over here?" I kick the dirt.

"This is where you piled them when they were too sick and the little ones died, like that one spring so many had pneumonia. Remember, here?"

Grace looks confused, but she keeps walking and touching things, old fences and the cracked paint on the buildings. This is good. This will help.

"Remember that?" I say, and point.

Grace follows my finger.

"That's where you parked the dead truck, and the weeds grew tall and came through the engine and we always talked about starting a garden there, growing tomatoes where the radiator would have been."

I can hear a voice far behind us, but don't look back. I take Grace's hand, and quicken.

"And the chute, do you remember the chute? Where we loaded pigs for sale and that one summer I was so sick of how it looked and I painted it bright yellow? And I painted all those flowers on it but all the flowers faded and there were only stems and it looked like I had painted weeds or prairie grass?"

"Do you remember here?" I say. I am shouting now and almost crying, and waving my hands in the air and waving Grace's, too. "This is where I rode my bike and that's where I fell off once and sprained my ankle. And you made me get on again and ride over that spot, shouting *You cannot stop me! I am victorious!* And my foot hurt so bad, pedaling, but I did feel it, I did feel victorious. I was unstoppable."

I pull her along faster, away from the voice as it gets closer.

"Excuse me? Can I help you?"

"Remember this, Grace? Do you remember this? This is where the lightning struck, right there, when I was eleven. It burned down the small barn in a moment, before we could even see it up in flames from the house, and it was going to take the whole farm. Do you remember?"

I point. I kick the ground.

"Do you remember, Grace?"

"And you wouldn't let me get close. All I could do was run back and forth with the buckets, back and forth with three, then four, carrying as fast as I could. And it was still raining and thundering and there was still lightning all around us. And you fought the fire by yourself, Grace. Do you remember that? And you won, you put it out. You saved us."

The burned-down barn isn't there anymore, just a patch of dirt between one new nursery and another. I get on my knees and try to uncover what I know has to be there somewhere, even if it was deep. The fire had scorched the ground, blackened it so that we saw it, changed, every day after. I dig fast in the dirt.

"Help me, Grace," I say, and tug her down so that she is kneeling and padding at the soil beside me.

"Who are you?" I hear. *"Hey! Can you hear me? What are you doing here?"*

"Remember, Grace. Please help me remember," I say, tears spilling over my eyes, making a mess of my vision. I can't see, but I don't stop digging.

"Remember?"

Then again, close enough to touch me: *"Hey? Who are you?"*

I can't face him, not yet. Through my blurry eyes, I can see Grace and we're so close that we're almost there. And then I scrape back another crust of dirt and I see it. Something twists in her face like recollection. A memory or a thought or a dream catches at the edge of her eyes, then drops into them. She remembers. She remembers. That's all I need.

We can go now.

Moon Dance

Kaye Park Hinckley

Every night when she makes her rounds, she finds us watching the Georgia moon. We lie together in a single bed to catch the first inkling of its light, and nightly mark its swell from minuscule to magnificent. We tell her of its essence, that it is something much bigger and brighter than itself. She gives us a condescending "Uh-huh, Shugah," then leans over to tuck the white sheet around our thighs and brush a dark hand across our foreheads. She smells of honey.

In the darkness, we point out to her how the moon takes center stage to a sparkle of dancing stars, how it soon becomes distorted, fades, and passes, leaving only a promise of return. We tell her that return is certain—our covenant between nothing and everything, between life and death. But she only wrinkles her sweet black face and smiles, a tall silhouette against the silver light from the window.

"Night, night, Miz Anna," she says.

I expect her to give us a kiss goodnight, but instead she gives us a pill for pain. On her way out, she does not close the window. She does not shut our door. We do not allow her to do that, because we will not be fastened here forever.

The artificial light from the hall draws a triangular shape on the linoleum, piercing the soft splash of moonlight that spreads downward from the foot of our bed. The illumination of the hall is soon extinguished by a human hand, but we lie in a radiance the human hand does not control.

In the night, we speak of the covenant, the promise in death. I see its purpose. Death is passage. Death is close.

One hundred and six years old, both of us, we've held many who passed before us, held them in our arms as they took a last breath—parents, children, grandchildren, others we loved. I tell Will that God's desires are greater than our own. He accepts the truth in that. Then we speak of our daughter, our first child.

We were sixteen when she was born, and we named her Annalee: Anna after my own name, and Lee, the maiden name of Will's mother. We lost three other children after Annalee came to us; a girl, too small to be born, another from consumption when she was a month old, and a son, killed by the fever before he was two. But Annalee was different; we blamed cruelty for taking her, human malice with no face or name. And we cried, Who would do this?

When you are old, there are painful things to be remembered. In the moonlight, your page, your time on earth, will be read to you, all in one moment. Listen. In silence you will hear the story of your life and the whisperings of God leading you through it.

Annalee was a small-boned girl of five when she died. I used to watch her play with the dolls I made from corncobs wrapped with cotton. I made clothes for the dolls, too. With my passed-down needle and thimble and thread, I sewed smiles into their faces like my own mama had done for me, sweet-bowed smiles like Annalee's.

There were three dolls, a mama, a daddy, and a baby doll. She'd named them after the three of us—Will, Anna, and Little Annalee. Will chuckled over that. He liked it that his child thought so much of him. Having something named after him made him feel like a man when he was no more than a boy.

Annalee cared for those dolls as if each one had real life within it. At night, she made a place for them in her bed, the baby between the mother and father. Then she sang them to sleep. In the daytime, she carried all three wherever she went. She had them with her in the pocket of her pinafore when she died. Thank God, she had them with her.

The woods beyond our house were beautiful in the fall, bronze and gold from the oaks and viridian green from the pines. Their deep purple shadows spread over a carpet of brown straw: all lovely, but Annalee and I liked the tall pyracantha tree best, its fiery red berries on glossy leaves, like nature's decorated Christmas tree. The berries were poisonous, though, and the tree couldn't be climbed because of its thorns. Yet beneath its overhanging bough lay a perfect little room for playing house, for making up stories, for laughing and singing, for looking out and for feeling safe inside. It was not a place for a child to die, yet that cruelty came. God does not will cruelty. Always there comes justification.

When Will and I married, in 1917, his daddy gave us eighty acres of good farmland alongside Black Snake Creek, on the Georgia side of the Chattahoochee River. His daddy and his two brothers helped us build our house out of heart pine. It had a front porch and four rooms with a kitchen out back and an outhouse beyond that. My grandmother Mamma Fiddie sewed curtains and made mattresses for our bed. She had Old Chollie bring her from Cuthbert, forty miles in the wagon, and they stayed most of two weeks, Old Chollie chopping piles of wood for the winter and Mama Fiddie sewing and sewing. I missed them a good deal after they left.

Mamma Fiddie was my mama's mother. Phalba was her given name, but when they were children, Old Chollie called her Miz Fiddie, so the name stuck. She took me as hers when my own mama died of yellow fever. Mamma Fiddie was a Story before she married a Hornsby. She's the one who picked Will for me to marry, worked it out with Will's daddy, her second cousin once removed.

Families stayed close then, moved from place to place together. The Storys and the Hornsbys came together from South Carolina to south Georgia. And cousins often married cousins. But I must have been agreeable to Will; he's never seemed dissatisfied. As for myself, I couldn't have found a better man on my own: long-legged and tall, over six feet, with black curly hair and skin flushing pink at the sight of a girl undressing in front of him.

Sometimes I did that, just to see him flush. Then I'd giggle, and hug him, and push him down on the bed Mama Fiddie made for us, all soft with straw and peanut shells and such. And when the moonlight came through the window, silvering our skin, we rose together and danced. Oh, the joy God gave us in the warmth of each other's arms!

When Annalee was born, Will refused to be sent to the porch. He was there, right beside Aunt Sarah, Old Chollie's wife, so he could hear our baby's first cry. Mama Fiddie sent Aunt Sarah a month before the birth because she herself had come down with the cough and didn't want to spread it. Aunt Sarah rode a mule those forty miles from Cuthbert just to be with me. It was her sweet black face that Annalee saw when she opened her little eyes to the world. "Thank you, sweet Jesus," Aunt Sarah said, "for another child o' God."

We had kind neighbors all around us, except down creek, where the Samsons lived. Mr. Samson was a farmer, too, but Will said it was just a cover for bootlegging. There was no Mrs. Samson, only two colored men that helped Mr. Samson out, and his own three boys. One of his sons, the youngest, wasn't right, and the other two mean as snakes. Usually, we saw them only at church meetings, where the youngest son took pleasure in taunting Annalee, snatching her dolls and grinding them in the dirt beneath his boot while she cried. Mr. Samson did nothing to stop him, so there was more than one run-in between Will and that Samson boy.

The War Between the States was still fresh then. We were only a generation past being a conquered country, after all. Mama Fiddie lived through the defeat. She sent her husband and five sons to the war. Three of her sons were killed, one lost a leg, and one had his palate shot out and never spoke again. Only her husband was not wounded. He came back to work their land. But Mama Fiddie's husband had been a Confederate officer during the war. Afterward, when he refused to take the Oath of Allegiance to the Union, the government punished

him by taking all he had, three hundred acres on Broad River in South
Carolina, land their families had settled in 1755 and fought for in the
Revolution; and then he was put in prison, where he died alone.

When the Storys and Hornsbys left for southwest Georgia, Mama
Fiddie went with them. She packed up her two wounded sons, her two
little girls, and the few belongings she had left—some tattered cloth,
her needles, and a sterling silver thimble her husband had given her. She
hid the thimble from Union soldiers by sewing it into her petticoat; it
meant that much to her.

They left behind stolen farmland, their homes, schools and churches
burned to the ground, their livestock slaughtered, and passed similar
misfortunes all the way to the Chattahoochee. Oh, is it any wonder
that thorns of meanness and resentment pricked into their hearts, or
that Mama Fiddie daily sewed sorrow into her salvaged cloth, a tapestry,
knotted and tied with pictures of her beloved dead?

Even now, I am filled with bitterness, until Will touches my shoulder, curls his body around mine, and says, "It's more a wonder that
kindness can still be found in those same anguished hearts."

His heart is good. He has forgiven the transgressions of others
against him, yet he will not trust that he, himself, can be forgiven—for
Will once killed an innocent man. He's still swaddled by the shadow
of his sin.

I kiss the nape of Will's neck, remembering when he wasn't here
beside me, but alone in the room across the hall. One evening he simply
appeared in my doorway, taut and dark-haired and smiling, as on those
first Sunday nights of our marriage, when I tugged him from our bed to
dance with me in the moonlight, a boy in love with the girl who loved
him.

Beyond his shoulder, I see Mama Fiddie's sterling silver thimble. It
sits where I have put it, between the windowpane and its wooden sill,
to keep from locking out all that passes in this world. For years, I have
taken the thimble from the cloth I wrapped it in—the tapestry sewn
with pictures of those gone before us—and placed it there. In the light

of each rising moon, it appears like a tiny beacon, pointing to a place where time is present.

When the moon is full, I lift the window high above the shining thimble that helped embroider our pasts and say to Will, Come. Dance with me in the moonlight.

He refuses. Always, he refuses.

Morning, we position ourselves just so we can see into the hall, but no one "out there" can gawk at us. Let them come inside if they want to see that we're still breathing. We watch the sun spread across the grass, browned from the drought of this Georgia summer. Will says there'll be no harvest for those who farm, no peanuts, no cotton, no keep for their families. There will be suffering.

At times, it was the same for us. We waited for water. We grieved for our lost children. We suffered. We prayed. And we did not die. In the end, our crops were given rain, and we were given one more child, who lived long enough to have a son himself.

She comes again, the sweet black face, to bring our breakfast, to give more pills. She is kind, but we will not get attached to her. The nice ones never stay long.

"Your grandson's here," she says cheerfully.

We hear his familiar footsteps, quick and purposeful. Our grandson has set a mission for himself. He is writing our history because he wants to know his own. His long, thin shape is framed between the wall of our room and the door's edge. "Good morning, Mamaw," he says. His hair has become white. How can it be?

Our grandson is a lawyer who defends the guilty. He is an advocate of mercy. He kisses my face, but does not kiss Will, though his grandfather leans toward him. Our grandson has a tape recorder stuck in a bulky bag that he sets on the waxed linoleum. He has Will's almond eyes and his smile is sweet, same as when Will held him cautiously in the old cane rocker, like silk in his arms, and sang to him, a newborn baby with no father, his mother gone crazy over the news of her husband's death.

The telegram came just as the war was over, the day the boy was born. *"We regret to inform you that . . ."* His father, the only child left to us, killed in the islands of the Pacific. His mother took her love letters, her two older girls, and disappeared forever. But she left her infant boy with us. We fed him, clothed him, read to him. We gave him all we knew of the chapter titles of life. Now, he wants to fill in the words.

I smell his cologne as he leans forward to pull his bulky bag closer. "You've been so good about telling the stories, Mamaw. Will you tell me about Annalee's murder?" He asks this so suddenly, I take in a breath.

He lays a hand on mine. "After all these years, I mean to solve it, once and for all. I'd like you to tell me what you remember." He is a determined lawyer, after all.

"Let your grandfather tell it," I whisper, my words weak, barely audible. I look at Will.

Our grandson seems startled, then grieved. "Mamaw, you know Granddaddy died ten years ago, in the room across the hall."

He most certainly did not. He's right here, beside me.

If our grandson was a boy again, I'd swat his bottom for lying.

He gently squeezes my fingers. There are tears in his eyes. "If you're not well, I'll come back another time."

No, don't leave. I turn to Will and see him hesitate; still I insist. "Your grandfather will tell you what you want to know."

My husband rises slowly from the bed and sits in the vinyl chair, his muscular thighs pressed against the cold firmness, a strand of hair, shiny as a blackbird's wing, tumbling onto his smooth forehead. He gives me a look of pain that calls for help.

Our grandson's eyes follow me as I sit next to Will in the cold vinyl chair. His body warms me as it has for the ninety years of our marriage. I've never regretted those years. Even when he failed, I forgave him. Forgiveness is required after a promise. At least, it used to be so.

Our grandson unzips his bulky bag to click on the tape recorder. I notice the small dimple on his chin, exactly like Will's. "Tell me what you remember about Annalee's death." He says this judiciously. I know he will not stay unless we do.

Will tenses beside me. He appears overcome, as if I should speak for him. And so, I try to.

I thought he would never get over it, the morning we found her little body beneath the pyracantha. Will held her to his heart, gave one long moan, then his sorrow turned to rage. His child was dead! He was certain it was the youngest Samson boy, the one stupid from birth, who strangled Annalee for no reason. So Will lynched him: an innocent man, but Will didn't know it when he strung him up.

Our grandson acts as if he hasn't heard a word I've said, as if we are just beginning our conversation. "I was once told that Grandfather hanged an innocent man," he says, fiddling with the tape recorder. He waits for my response. I give him a nod.

Our grandson, a lawyer who argues for reprieve, shakes his head reproachfully. It is a reaction I did not expect. As if such a thing has never before happened on earth. As if mercy—the virtue that commits our grandson to his profession—had died, then and there, on the cross of Christ. As if innocent Jesus Himself hadn't been the victim of angry men, yet asked His Father's forgiveness of his murderers. I am disappointed in the dearth of compassion from my own kin.

Will looks down. I'm certain he is recalling the man's last pitiful gasp for life as he swung from the limb of a tree. I am certain he is chastising himself for his fury that took an innocent life. When I reached him that night, he was on his knees beneath the tree, crying inconsolably. Two deaths, already, in that one day; I worried there would be three.

But our grandson is waiting for me to speak.

We had a beautiful funeral for Annalee, nice funerals for all our children, but for Annalee we tried to make it special so maybe she could see from heaven that kindness is often returned with kindness, that there is more goodness in the world than meanness. A person has to believe that, or all around him will be dark. God is in the span of time between darkness and light. Little by little, like the moon, He shows His reflection and waits to be invited to the dance.

Then my own tears come. I can't hold them back. Our grandson comes toward me, puts an arm around my shoulders. "We don't have to talk today, Mamaw."

Oh, but I do. At first Will believed what he'd done was right, but in the days that followed, we learned the truth. Despite its thorns, Annalee had climbed the tree and had broken her neck when she fell from it. It was then I saw enough torment in Will's face to last a lifetime, enough that he confessed his violence, enough that he asked pardon of the bootlegger, Samson, for the lynching of his son. Of course, Mr. Samson gave no pardon, but there was compassion from a jury. Still, Will spent five years in prison.

Our grandson empathizes with my tears, but strokes my arm as if I've said nothing. "Besides your husband, you lost your children, all except my dad," he murmurs, as if he's talking to himself.

Why won't you listen? I accepted Annalee's death long ago, and the deaths of my other children, too! (Have I snapped at him?) I know they are with God. It's your grandfather I'm worried about. He paid a penalty on earth for what he did and begged God's mercy. Yet now he despairs that God could love him enough to forgive him.

"Separation from those we love is hard," our grandson says.

I try to shout: Pity your grandfather! Be God's advocate!

Except I hear no words come from my mouth.

Our grandson says, "You're too weak to talk now, Mamaw. I'll come again when you're stronger."

I don't want him to leave. I want him to live up to his vocation. But he kisses me, and is gone.

All seems just as it was before our grandson came. Inside the air remains cool, and the artificial plants have no thirst in a world that desires nothing except to be kept from discomfort, a world that doesn't acknowledge how suffering can be wisdom's light at work, and that out of his weakness, a sinner can become the beacon he was meant to be.

Except it is not as it was. Will turns his boyish eyes to the opened, paned window. Beyond it, the sun infuses our guarded ground with an eclipse of cross-shaped shadows to cool it. The cones of a long-leafed pine, like multiple crown of thorns, have fallen into a bed of zinnias and daisies, their stems bent in authentic thirst until a gardener who is picking up the cones sees the need and waters them. Azaleas, without blooms, their leaves the color of a faded dollar bill, still continue to champion the walkway. A hungry blackbird pecks the pavement, finding only pebbles, until another, with a red berry in its beak, comes to compensate. Will watches the two fly off together, then turns to me. In his once hopeless expression, I see a small change.

I remind him of another summer without water, the drought from which God saved us. I remind him that after we had suffered through it all, new life grew within me. I tell him to expect the same. Then I touch his shoulder.

He ponders my words.

The moon is rising now. Again, she comes to make her rounds. Her kind, dark hands give us a pill, but as we thought, at the end of the week she will leave here for good to make her way in a better place.

Will takes my hand and says that it's time for us to leave here, too. We follow the silver ribbon of light to the window, the way out from this world. The light traces the turn of Will's face, caresses the slope of his shoulders, and a boy of sixteen embraces the girl who has loved him for decades.

Come, Will, I say. Dance with me in the moonlight.

This time, he doesn't refuse.

True or False

Bernard Scott

The priests at St. Andrew's were still in the habit of hearing confessions before the five-thirty Mass on Saturday, though not every Saturday, the way it was in former times. Hardly anyone now ever came except old ladies who used to belong to the altar society, and very occasionally a parishioner with some sort of real problem, usually of a domestic turn not having anything to do with serious sin exactly. And sometimes a stranger would enter the confessional, someone whose voice the priest had never heard before, someone perhaps from a neighboring parish hoping for more anonymity than the confessional screen in the home parish could afford. These cases would generally involve something more recognizable as sin and perhaps for this reason were pretty rare.

Given all this, Father Louis Reilly, pastor of St. Andrew's, decided confessions need only be heard before the five-thirty Mass every other Saturday. His assistant, Father Timothy O'Connell, the parochial vicar, certainly had no problem with this arrangement. After all, Father Tim reasoned, people with a pressing problem on those off-Saturdays could always call the rectory and make an appointment.

That's just what happened on one of those Saturdays. It was close to five o'clock and Father Reilly, who had the five-thirty that particular Saturday, was in his study with the door closed. Father Tim was already dressed in sweater and jeans for an evening out and was about to leave

41

when the phone on his desk rang.

"Confessions are held on the first and third Saturdays," he said when he heard the reason for the call.

"To tell you the truth, I really don't know if any of the parishes are hearing confession today," he answered pleasantly, his foot up on the desk. "Probably not this late," he added, noticing a spot of something on his new Reeboks.

"Well, it is pretty late now," Father Tim said, looking at his watch.

"No!" he said laughing. "We don't hear confessions over the telephone. That's one thing we can't do, at least not yet!" He laughed again.

"Well," he said, "is it something that can't really wait? How about tomorrow before Mass maybe?"

"No, sure, fine, no, hey it's okay," he said, his voice masking the sour look on his face. "Are you nearby?"

"All right, just come to the rectory," he said. "I'm Father Tim. I'll be here."

He hung up and immediately dialed another number.

"Joe," he said, "I've gotten tied up here for a bit. No, I don't think so. Maybe ten, twenty minutes tops. If it's more than that, you guys go ahead. I'll catch up with you at the restaurant. And save some calamari for me," he added with a laugh, then hung up.

A thick-set, blue collar gent in his early forties arrived ten minutes later, looking rather glum. "Shall we go into my office?" Father Tim asked, pointing to a door. "Or we could go over to the confessional in the church. Suit yourself. We still have a few minutes before the five-thirty."

"This is okay," the penitent said, moving to the office.

"I haven't been to confession for a while," the man said when they were seated.

"That's no problem," Father Tim said with a wave of his hand. He liked to get people to relax.

"It's been a real long while," the man said.

"Well, how long?"

"About twenty years, maybe longer," the man said.

"Well," said Father Tim with a nod, "at least you're here now. That's good."

"We're supposed to go once a year, isn't that right?" the man asked.

"Yes," Father Tim said. "Gets things off your chest. You married?"

"Yeah," the man said.

"So," Father Tim said, shifting, "what's on your mind?"

"I'd like to go to confession," the man repeated.

"Right." Father Tim hesitated. He noticed the man was staring at the Reeboks. "Let me get my stole," Father Tim said. He got up and rummaged through a closet. "It's in here somewhere," he said absently. After half a minute more of rummaging, he suddenly stopped. "Ah," he said, hitting his hand to his head, "my bedroom closet. Be right back."

He returned a minute later.

"So now," Father Tim said, slipping back into his seat, his purple stole slung incongruously down around a green turtleneck and a blue-green sweater. "Shall we start?" He gestured when the man didn't say anything.

At length the man said, "Help me out, Father. It's been so long. Isn't there something special I'm supposed to say to get started?"

"Well," Father Tim said with an effort to smile, "you usually tell the priest how long it's been since your last confession. But you've already done that."

The man sat forward a little. "I remember it," he said, his face brightening with a smile. "Bless me, Father, for I have sinned. It's been twenty years since my last confession."

"Very good," said Father Tim. "Just go ahead now. Tell me what's bothering you."

"I don't know how to say this, Father," the man said. "It's hard for me."

"Well, something is bothering you, right?"

"Yes, Father, definitely."

"Can you tell me what it is?"

"That's just it, Father. I'm having trouble finding the words."

"Have you committed some sin?"

"Like fornication, Father?"

"Fornication, whatever."

"Not really, Father. I don't screw around or anything like that. I look at the girls at the plant once in a while maybe the way I shouldn't, but not really. I mean I don't do things with them in my mind, like. You know what I mean? Maybe I used to but I'm past that sort of stuff now. Getting too old for one thing."

"You said you're married?"

"Yes, Father."

"Well, is everything all right there? Are you fighting with your wife?"

"Nah, we hardly talk to each other. I mean we get along okay. She stays in her corner, I stay in mine. I'm married almost twenty years, Father. I've already said everything I'm gonna say to her probably a hundred times over."

"Okay. Well, where does it hurt? as the doctor said. Something's bothering you, it seems."

"What's sin, Father?"

Father Tim blinked and tried not to smile. "That's a good question actually," he said. "I often ponder that myself," he added with a laugh.

"Sin is you go against the Ten Commandments. Right?"

"That's a good place to start," Father Tim said.

"I don't steal, I don't really lie much, I don't hurt anybody, I don't fornicate. Does that mean I'm not a sinner?"

"Hey, I'm just a priest, not a judge. That's the job of your conscience. I can see that something's bothering you."

"Yeah, but I can't put my finger on it exactly. I thought maybe you could help me."

Father Tim hesitated for a moment. "Sin," he said, "is something you do that is against your own best interests. That's the bottom line. You sin when you do something that hurts you yourself, the inner you."

"What about others, what about God, Father?"

"Well, when you sin against others, you hurt them, but who are you really hurting? You hurt yourself. You can't hurt God, right? If you cheat on your wife or something like that, who's getting hurt the most in the final analysis, you or her? You. You hurt the relationship. You destroy your right to that relationship. That's the bottom line far as I can see."

"What if you kill somebody? It's the other person dies, not you."

"Well, you can take a person's life but not his soul. But a person who does that could be destroying his own soul."

"I see what you're getting at, Father. Maybe that's what's bothering me." He paused for a moment and then asked, "Do you have a Bible, Father?"

"I have one right here, as a matter of fact," the priest said, taking one from his desk.

"Could I see it, Father?" the man said.

The priest handed him the Bible.

"Father, I never read this thing but the other day I picked it up and just started with the first page. I read about Adam and Eve and the Garden, you know." The man leaned forward. "They committed the first sin, right?" he asked.

"We don't know exactly," the priest said. "It's a story meant for our instruction."

"A story, Father?" the man asked. "You're saying none of this happened? I think you're wrong there, Father. It happened. It says so right here."

Father Tim looked at his watch. "You know," he said, "you've caught me at a bad time. I was just on my way out. We could talk about this some other time."

The man seemed not to hear. "And there's this tree in the middle of the garden," he continued. He had opened the Bible and was pointing to a page in the early chapters of Genesis.

"The tree of the knowledge of good and evil," the priest said mechanically.

"Yeah, that one too. But this other tree, in the exact middle of the garden, Father, the tree of life. What's that all about, Father?"

"You know we should talk about this some other time," Father Tim said, making as if to stand.

"And after they sinned," the man went on, "God puts this angel in front of the tree with a flaming sword so nobody can get at it. Why'd he do that, Father? Isn't God supposed to be a good guy? I mean everybody else does things like that to protect their turf, but why God? He's supposed to love us, right?"

"Look," the priest said more severely, "I really have to go."

"Just let me get this off my chest, okay, Father?"

"Okay, sure," Father Tim said obligingly, after a moment's hesitation, recovering his sense of priestly duty. "No problem." He sank back in his chair and reflected for a moment. "The Tree of Life is a figure of speech, I suppose," he said to the man. "The writer had to explain the presence of death in a world that God created and said was good."

"So he puts that flaming sword there so we couldn't eat the apples or whatever from that tree, so we would die? Is that the idea?"

"Well, there's got to be some connection between sin and death," Father Tim said, trying to hold his own interest. "This is pretty abstract stuff. Is this what you came to see me about?"

"No, Father. I just wondered about it. Like there's something missing in my life. Maybe God's just blocking it off from me."

"What do you mean by 'it'?"

"Life, Father. Real life. You know what I mean? Half the time I feel like something that's gone sour in the fridge, like I been just rotting away most of my life. I never seen nothing, nothing you could really call life. Did you ever think we're all rotting apples? Know what I mean?"

"I'm not sure I follow you exactly," the priest said.

"Well, Father, take today. I get up at seven. I eat breakfast. My wife doesn't talk to me except to remind me to take out the garbage. The kids are fighting. I start out the day yelling. My wife makes a face and goes upstairs. I have to make my own sandwich. And this is supposed to be my home. A man's home, you know?" The man shook his head. "I can't even take the couple of dollars to buy a sandwich 'cause I got to replace the roof this year and there's no way I'm gonna be able to do that."

"Where do you work?" the priest asked, hoping to move the conversation along.

"You mean where did I work," the man said.

"You're unemployed?"

"I lost my job today."

"You got laid off?"

"I got fired. I called my boss a stupid jerk. Something worse, actually."

"You know, this isn't exactly a confessional matter." The priest looked at his watch and stood up. "You need to talk to somebody who can help you with these problems."

"I need absolution, Father."

The priest stood there for a moment looking at him. The man was bent over, plowing callused fingers through thick, rough hair just beginning to gray around the edges. "What have you done?" the priest asked eventually.

The man looked up at the priest and gave him a strange smile. He picked up the Bible and flipped to the back. "Here, Father. In the last chapter of the Bible, in the book of Revelation, Christ is talking about this tree again, the Tree of Life. The same tree. It's the first time we hear of it since Genesis. I looked. It ain't nowhere else in the Bible I could see. It's in Genesis, right at the beginning of the Bible, and it comes up again on the very last page. It ain't anyplace else. Just at the beginning and end, right?"

"I'm not really sure."

"Believe me, Father. I went through it last night. But it's at the beginning and at the end of the Bible. So it's got to be pretty important, right, Father?"

The priest sat down again and was peering at the man. "I have to go," he said quietly. "If you want to talk about these things, we can do it some other time. Make an appointment. I'd be happy to chat with you."

"I'll tell you what I think, Father," the man said, oblivious to the priest's restlessness. "Look, here's what Jesus said. He says he's the beginning and the end, and that he's coming soon and he's going to pay every man for what he's done. But he says the ones who wash their robes will be able to eat from the Tree of Life and enter the new city by the gates. You read it too, right, Father?" he asked, handing the priest the Bible.

The priest took the Bible and looked at the passage.

"Right there, Father," the man said, getting up from his seat and pointing at the passage in question. "Ain't that something? There's gonna be this new Jerusalem that will come right down from heaven, all shining with diamonds and precious jewels and stuff. It looks like the angel is still there guarding everything but now he lets certain people through. These are the good guys, the ones who cleaned up their act. They can walk right in and eat from that tree all they want."

He sat down and shook his head. Neither of them moved for a time, and then the man said to the priest, "Any of this make sense to you, Father?" The priest looked at him curiously and said nothing.

"Let me have that for a moment, will you, Father?" the man said, reaching for the Bible. "Here's the other side of the story. It says that certain kinds of people will be kept out. That angel ain't gonna let them in." He began to read. "'Outside are the dogs and sorcerers and fornicators and murderers and idolaters . . .'" The man stopped reading and looked up. "No problem for us there, right, Father?" he said with a wink and a smile.

The priest looked at him and said nothing.

"But here's this other thing, Father. This is the part that gets to me. Those who have led a 'false life' will also be kept outside, along with the dogs and fornicators." The man studied the priest. "What's that mean to you, Father? 'A false life.'"

The priest blinked and started to say something but stopped. "It could mean a number of things," he said after a moment.

"Anyway, Father, can I have your absolution?"

"Sure, but you have to tell me some sin first, okay?" the priest said.

"I just did."

"What sin was that?" the priest said.

"A false life, Father. That's me. I've been living a false life. I'm one of those guys."

"Okay. Right. But can you be a little more specific? False in what way?"

"I'll be specific, Father. My life stinks. Lately I look at myself when I'm shaving and want to throw up." He rubbed his hand across his chin. "I'll give you details, Father. I get up in the morning. It starts there. I go to work, glad to get out of the house. I get to the plant and wonder how there could be such stupid people in the world. I'm talking about my boss. Lunchtime I throw away my dumb sandwich and spend five dollars I don't have on a beer and a plate of spaghetti at a diner down the street from the plant. In the afternoon my boss tells me I didn't do something the way he said and I tell him it was dumb to do it that way. He tells me I'm going to do it his way anyway, and I tell him he has his head up . . . you know where."

"So it's your anger that bothers you?"

"Naw, I wasn't angry. I was just mad. He was partly right, you know. I knew that. I didn't like him coming up to me that way, that's all."

"So you want to confess a sin of pride?"

"Father, I want to confess I been living a false life. That's my sin. I can see it."

"I'm having trouble with what you mean by a false life."

"I just told you Father—*my* life.

Father Tim's gaze began to drift past the man.

"Father"—the man pushed on—"do you believe there's such a thing as this Tree of Life?"

"Sure. As a figure of speech, I guess I do."

"Do you think that 'figure,' or whatever you call it, is going to be for you?"

"I certainly hope so."

"Me too," he said. "So how about it, Father?"

The priest looked at him uncertainly.

"Absolution, Father, absolution."

The priest, seeking some definite matter he could legitimately absolve, asked the man, "You're sorry for the sins of your past life, correct?"

"You bet, Father."

"What about anger?"

"Anger, everything, Father. The whole kit and caboodle."

The priest smiled, hesitated for a moment, then raised his hand and slowly began to recite the words of absolution.

The man interrupted him at once. "Father, excuse me. Don't I have to make an act of contrition? I want to do this right."

"If you wish. My feeling is that just your coming in here is an act of contrition."

"I'd like to do this the way I was taught as a kid, Father. But I don't remember how it goes."

"Just tell God you're sorry. That will be enough."

The man hesitated. "Okay, Father, if you say so." He knelt in front of the priest and began to pray. "I'm sorry, Lord. I'm sorry for being a phony, for living what you call a false life. Lord, forgive me. Jesus, help me to be different. Give me a real life."

"Okay, that's good," the priest said. He recited the words of absolution, making the sign of the cross.

"I think God is pleased with you," he said, putting his hand on the man's shoulder.

"I'm clean," the man said with a broad smile. "It's been twenty years."

Father Tim helped the penitent get up. "God bless you," he said.

They each turned away and made moves to depart. The priest thoughtfully folded up his stole and placed it carefully on the desk. The man, his face shiny with joy, was on his way out when he stopped and turned back to the priest. "Father," he said, "there's something at the end of the Bible could be for you too." He picked up the book from the priest's desk, opened it, and pointed to a particular verse. "Read this sometime, Father," he said, thumping his finger on the page. "Maybe it's got your number."

They left, the penitent to his new life, the priest to Luigi's and his calamari. But the confession the priest heard stuck with him. He was uncharacteristically quiet that evening with his friends. They asked him if anything was wrong. He laughed it off, but he wasn't his usual cut-up self. When they broke up and he was back at the rectory, he went into his office and got the Bible. Before turning out his light, he turned to the the book of Revelation and looked up the passage he had been told had his number. It was virtually the last lines of Scripture, a sort of postscript the apostle had written to warn his readers.

"This is my solemn attestation to all who hear the prophesies in this book: if anyone adds anything to them, God will add to him every plague mentioned in this book; if anyone cuts anything out of the prophesies of this book, God will cut out his share of the tree of life and the holy city which are described in this book. The one who attests to these things says: I am indeed coming soon."

Father Tim read it twice. Was the passage supposed to be about him? Was he one of those who added something to the prophecies? Had he cut out anything? He didn't see it that way, but the priest didn't sleep well that night. His thoughts kept going back over his life. Was it a good life? Was his possibly a false life also? How many times had he mocked his superiors? Not in so many words perhaps. How long had it been since he had been to confession? He, a priest of God.

The following week was not a good one for Father Tim. "You all right, Tim?" Father Reilly asked him one morning, observing the younger priest over the top of his newspaper. The pastor liked his assistant but they never seemed to really connect. Different generations, different wavelengths. It made the older pastor a little sad.

"I'm fine," Father Tim lied.

"Sure? You look a little wan."

"No, everything's great. Guess I'm tired." He poured himself another cup of coffee.

"I can take the funeral this morning if you want," the pastor said.

"Thanks," Father Tim said, shaking his head and smiling. "I'm okay. Guess funerals aren't my thing," he added after a time.

The older priest, back into his newspaper, looked at his assistant for a second, made a sound in his throat, and went back to his reading.

"But that's what I'm here for," Father Tim said absently. He got up and went down the hall to his room.

The funeral was for a middle-aged woman who had died of cancer. Someone from the old neighborhood surrounding the church. She never came to St. Andrew's as far as he knew. She had three living children and they all had kids. Her oldest boy was killed in Vietnam. Father Tim saw someone in the pews who must have been the husband, along with what looked like scads of uncles and aunts, siblings, cousins and kids of all ages. There was a really old lady who could have been the grand-mother. The deceased woman must have been loved. Probably a terrific cook. A big woman in a big lively family, like in the old days. The kind they don't grow anymore.

"She was a good woman," Father Tim heard himself saying from the pulpit. "She lived a good life." He usually said that even if he knew nothing about the deceased. He could tell from the faces of the surviving family what kind of life the dead person had lived. Once he got into it, he knew he liked to preach. He liked reaching people. For him the homilies at Mass were more important, more real than the Sacrament. The Church is people, not sacraments, one of his seminary professors used to say, and he couldn't agree more. But today the words he was speaking seemed to fall flat. They left a bad taste in his mouth. What was going wrong with him?

At the cemetery after the interment, one of the family members came up to him. An uncle probably. Father Tim recognized his face. Back of the church at the seven-o'clock Mass Sunday mornings. Sometimes he ushered. The parishioner kept shaking his head as he told the priest about her end. "She wouldn't see anybody, Father," he said. "She was angry for a long time. At the end I think she was just scared.

She should have seen a priest. She didn't have the last rites, nothing."

"Wasn't she a good woman?" Father Tim asked.

"She was okay, Father, don't get me wrong. But she wasn't a happy person, know what I mean?"

"Seems like a good, happy family," the priest said.

"We got our share of problems, Father. Don't you kid yourself. People ain't themselves at funerals, know what I mean?"

"I suppose you're right."

"Pray for her, will you? And while you're at it, do me a favor, Father, and mention my name too, okay? I'm Anthony."

"Of course," Father Tim said. "Anthony." He had already forgotten the name of the deceased woman.

By the end of the week, Father Tim had a bad cold and headache that would not go away.

"I'll take the morning Mass," Father Reilly said at breakfast. It was Saturday and there was only the nine o'clock. "You go back to bed. Get some rest."

Father Reilly took confessions that afternoon too. It was Father Tim's turn but Father Reilly insisted. One of the altar ladies was already there waiting for him at four o'clock. She was there every month. The trouble this time was her daughter-in-law yelled at her and she gave it right back. It took all of about three minutes to get this off her chest and be absolved. After her there was no one, not for forty minutes. Father Reilly sat there in the reconciliation room and read his Office. He didn't mind the solitude. It was a pleasant little room. The late-afternoon sun shone behind a small stained-glass window, creating a lovely rainbow effect. The air in the room seemed liquid with colors. There was an empty chair for the penitent to sit facing him, and a chair behind a screen if the penitent needed privacy. Every few minutes Father Reilly turned the page of his breviary. He'd read a few lines and then close his eyes. Sometimes he couldn't tell if it was prayer or sleep. He felt at peace in a world he knew wasn't peaceful any more.

He must have been dozing just before the hour was up when the door to the confessional, which had been left ajar, opened wide. Father Tim was standing before him, looking forlorn and crumpled. Father Reilly looked up at him. "Tim," he said. "What's up?"

Father Tim exhaled a huge volume of air in a painful sigh and sat down heavily on the chair facing his boss. "This has been hell week," he said, shaking his head.

Father Reilly studied him for a moment. "Cold any better?"

"I'm in some kind of hole," Father Tim said. "I need something to get me out of this funk."

"Want to talk?" Father Reilly asked, putting down his breviary.

Father Tim shook his head and looked at his boss. "I haven't been to confession for three years," he said meekly.

Father Reilly raised his eyebrows and nodded. "That's too long," he said.

"Someone came in for confession last Saturday," Father Tim said. "He hadn't been to confession for twenty years. When he left with the absolution, he was like a new man. It was beautiful."

Father Reilly nodded and waited.

Father Tim looked at his boss with a kind of lame smile, leaned forward putting his head into his hands, and began speaking to the floor. "You and I kind of keep to ourselves," he said. "We don't talk much. Maybe we should. We sort of . . . stay in our own corners." He looked up at his boss. A soft light had crept into the eyes of the older priest. The colored light coming through the stained-glass window had painted his face in soft liquid hues. The old priest's face seemed to be glowing. The two men sat looking at each other in the silence of the little room for a long minute. Then the young priest slid to his knees.

"Bless me, Father, for I have sinned. It has been a whole lifetime since my last confession . . ."

Water

Michael Piafsky

To begin with, there was the bus ride, a long one. Our Lady of Lourdes was halfway across the city. They'd left early in the morning, early enough that there weren't any empty seats. A middle-aged man finally stood up and offered his place, folding his newspaper under his arm and nodding coldly as she sat. He looked straight ahead after that, never down at her, even when she'd told Jamey to thank the nice gentleman as she waved the infant's mittened hand. A woman across the aisle smiled at this and asked how old the baby was.

"Three months," Carol said.

"Cute," the woman said.

The man with the newspaper said nothing, and eventually moved up to the front of the bus to get off. Pretty sour, Carol thought. Nobody made him give up the seat, although who's kidding whom? She had scanned the rows for a likely candidate, walking past three old women in plastic raincoats too thin for January and a high school kid with an iPod blaring music she could hear four seats down. So maybe he was justified, but he gave up his seat regardless and Carol thought in this case that was more important. Whoever said it was the thought that counts sure wasn't living in this world.

By the time she got off, near Manchester Square the bus was nearly empty. Most of the crush had tumbled out of the bus downtown at the giant office complexes while the old women had gotten off en masse, shrieking at the driver to stop in front of a bakery. He'd jolted the bus to a halt and the women had to hold on to each other for balance. When the doors opened, they created a wind tunnel and Carol tilted Jamey's head forward into her breast to muffle the bite. She could hear the sound of a horn and, looking out the window, saw a red sports car pull up alongside the bus, its driver raising his free hand in protest. The bus driver didn't respond. He just pulled the doors shut.

If Del had been there, he would have been unhappy with the bus driver. He would have bent over and whispered into Carol's ear that the sports car had a point. Buses cannot simply stop in the middle of the street because it happens to suit some old women. That it was cold would not have mattered to Del. The ice, the uneven pavement, arthritis, all of these would have sounded like weak alibis to him—in perfect health save constant eye strain and the beginnings of a bad back. Sitting on the cold plastic bench, Carol found herself getting unhappy at Del's selfishness, but he wasn't there to prolong the imaginary argument, so it died prematurely.

They'd been fighting more. The new pressures of the baby were getting to both of them. Del started coming home from the office later and later, almost as late as he had before she had gotten swollen with the pregnancy. Carol couldn't decide if it was stress at trying to provide for the future or unhappiness with the whole situation. The advice she read from her magazines wavered on this point too. Ultimately, Del wasn't there for most anything and Carol would jam the marching hordes of laundry into the machine with genuine rage, dispensing capfuls of Dreft like weapons of mass destruction. Jamey, wobbling in his bouncy chair in the doorway, would puzzle at her when she transferred the load into the dryer, and recoil when she kicked the door shut.

"Let his lordship work till midnight to pay for a new one," she'd hiss, then feel bad at seeing new dents in the door. Not that Del had ever noticed and the dryer was still working, so no major harm done.

By and large, Del was content to let most of the responsibilities slide to her. He had an infuriating knack for assuming to know what was important and what wasn't. When she'd phoned the Montessori pre-school to sign Jamey up, Del sat there with a bemused expression on his face. "It's four years from now," Del said. "The kid can't hold his head up yet and you've got him enrolled in preschool."

"When would you suggest I do it?" Carol snapped. "You'll notice that they took the call. The receptionist wrote him down in the book, told me she'd send me the appropriate forms. I mean, they weren't surprised."

"It seems strange to me, off somewhere in the future," Del said and smiled weakly, and it might have ended there but Jamey started cry-ing and Carol could see Del's head twitch back toward her. She waited statue-still until he finally picked up Jamey and began juggling him between his arms. Carol called back the woman at the preschool and asked how many children were already enrolled for Jamey's year.

"Seven," Carol informed Del. Then she walked past him on her way to the bedroom. She stopped and wrinkled her nose. "He needs to be changed."

Carol waited by the bedroom door and watched in the reflection from a picture frame as Del carried Jamey into the nursery. He was car-rying him like a football. Carol was hopeful in thinking about how much the diaper must have shifted with Del's rough play and was grati-fied a few moments later to hear Del's curses. She went into the bath-room and locked the door.

As she stood before the mirror, she had to admit to herself that Del was conscientious in the beginning. After all, he had escorted the two of them to the pediatrician's office the first few appointments, and read pamphlets in the waiting room. Now he was obsessed with vacci-nations and immunizations. "We owe it to him," he'd explained to her. He compiled a list and was running down the horrible diseases with a pen. When she complained that some of these might be a little prema-ture, he listed symptoms. "Body ache, rash, pitted scars," he said, primly. "Thirty percent risk of death." His voice dropped ridiculously at that last word.

"When?" she'd asked. "Name someone who recently died of smallpox."

He just stood there, his pen perched at the midpoint of the paper.

"It's a lot of needles," she said.

"Better safe than sorry," he said. "What can it hurt?"

At least Jamey wasn't adding to the troubles. He was a good child, getting stronger every day. He didn't have any health issues, pronounced healthy both by her pediatrician and by her mother. This was on Thanksgiving, the kid only three weeks old and beet red. Del was talking about jaundice, lecturing to the extended family on bilirubin counts and prenatal nutrition. He'd been reading again.

At Thanksgiving, Carol was thankful for her mother. Must have been the first time since she was six or seven she felt that way. Now widowed, her mother lived in one of the suburbs and what had seemed horribly close for the first five years of Carol's marriage now seemed god-sent. For all of her mother's faults, and Carol could enumerate these at high speed, the woman knew enough to keep a baby alive for three hours while Carol got her hair done or went to the bank. Which was more than could be said about Del, who would declare himself unready whenever she ventured that an hour outside might be nice for her. "I'm still learning," he'd say, as if this excused his incompetence. How hard was it? If her mother's spaniel had thumbs, Carol would have left Jamey with her.

So on Thanksgiving, Carol was thankful, for her own mother, for Jamey's health, and, sure, for the steady money from Del's job. She was thankful for their apartment, and central heating and disposable diapers. She was thankful that Del's parents lived in Phoenix, at a golf course community, and rarely asked Del to put her on the phone. Del's mother was a tiny woman. Her body was so slight that Carol couldn't imagine how she'd ever had Del. The only thing Del's mother ever said about childbirth was that she'd left the hospital a size four. "They told us to put on less weight then, dear," she'd said. Del had been raised by a steady stream of nannies, from more or less impoverished countries. Left alone with him, Del's mother used to prod him with a broom handle.

So maybe all of it wasn't Del's fault, but this certainly didn't comfort her any.

And yet there were times when it seemed like they were close to something. One Friday afternoon, in her seventh month, Del had surprised her coming home early with a bucket of red paint and some thin artist's brushes. Then he held up a single finger and disappeared into the brownstone's tiny nursery. She'd chosen the nursery color herself, a neutral violet, and for a second she was angry, viewing the paint as another implied criticism. But instead Del reappeared with an oversized book. "I got it from the library," he explained. "Magical creatures, look."

And together they'd gone through and selected figures to trace onto the baby's walls. There were animals from all over the world and they leafed through the pages eliminating the most fearsome and the most silly. In the end they'd agreed on a centaur and a gryphon, a unicorn and a chimaera. Then Del pulled a piece of paper from his pocket and unfolded it on the floor. It was a large dragon, with hairy eyebrows and a drooping mustache.

"I'm not sure about that one," Carol said in a steady voice. "That might scare the baby."

"No it won't," Del argued. "Dragons are not frightening creatures, they're noble and wise."

"You're trying to tell me that these don't look frightening?" she said, pointing to sharpened talons curving over a forked tail.

"Saint George sold you all a bill of goods," Del said. "This dragon is Asian." He smiled and pointed to its eyes. "Just like mine," he said and winked. "Very wise."

"Wise or not, it's going to be terrifying." She felt bad about it. Del almost never said anything about his heritage. Her mother still made spaetzle at Christmas time and talked about relatives in from Munich. If Del had any relatives left in Korea, neither he nor his family ever mentioned them. She felt bad but she was right.

"Paint what you want," she'd finally said, unwilling to exhaust all of their good feelings. "But you're going to explain to your child that dragons don't eat babies."

"I'll do one better," Del said, grinning. He pulled out a second sheet with a beautiful bird in flight. "It's a phoenix," he said. "A protector to go above the crib." He squeezed her hand. "It'll be perfect," he said. "You'll see."

From Manchester Square, it was a short walk to the church. She repositioned herself on the curb. It was now middle morning but still no sun. People were saying it was unusually cold for early January but Carol couldn't really tell. She'd been in the house so long that her breath was taken away the second she'd stepped onto the sidewalk in front of her brownstone. Jamey didn't seem to mind, though she noticed his cheeks plumped up. He stared directly up at the milky sky until he drifted into sleep.

There must have been a hundred churches between their walk-up and Our Lady of Lourdes, many of them Catholic, but her mother wanted the ceremony done in her church. She said she was friendly with one of the priests there, and a long bus ride didn't seem reason enough to tell her no. Her mother promised to meet her there to facilitate, which was nice because heaven knows Carol had no clue how to go about any of it.

Besides, it never would have done to go to the church half a block from her house. Not that Del had ever been inside, nor she herself for that matter, but still, they knew people who went. People who would tell Del they'd seen her and Jamey. No reason for them not to, really. Who would think you'd have to go skulking around just to get a baby baptized?

At first it was an idle thought, something she'd skimmed past at breakfast one morning, Del with one foot out the door. He'd laughed, told her he'd fend for himself for dinner. That night, in bed, she'd felt for his naked leg with her hand and asked again.

"Absolutely not" he said, clearly surprised that she should bring up such a ridiculous thing for a second time.

"Why not?" she asked. "It might be nice. An excuse for pictures, at the very least."

"Did your mother put you up to this?" he said, his eyes narrowing. Her mother was suddenly practicing again after many decades of lapse. Before Carol herself had been born, they'd given it up and now her mother was back attending Sunday Mass and the occasional Friday-night Adoration. It was another constant, if subterranean, source of chafing between Carol and Del, who tended toward suspicion about his mother-in-law's motives and never missed an opportunity to point out that Carol was too quick to succumb to her hectoring.

"Why not?"

"Witchcraft," he said, turning over onto his shoulder.

It remained like this for a few minutes, Carol getting angrier and angrier, until Jamey started to cry for his bottle. "I'll get it," Del said with a loud sigh, and she followed him across the hall to the nursery.

"I don't see why we can't talk about this," she said.

He spun around and Carol watched Jamey's eyes widen, his cries warping with the Doppler effect. "We did talk about this. Remember?"

And to be fair, they had. Early on in the pregnancy, Del had taken out a pad of paper and written down their views on key issues. Breast-feeding (absolutely), family bed (absolutely not). Religion was down near the bottom of the list. At the time, Carol was drowsy and her bladder was ready to burst. They'd agreed on a course of inaction. If the kid wanted to do something later in life, they'd support that, but no sense in encouraging anything. No sense in begging for trouble, Del had said.

Later she'd brought it up again and Del walked out of the room. "He'll probably get an earful no matter what school we send him to. You want the kid believing that stuff?"

"It's a baptism, for God's sake," she said, following him down the narrow hallway. "We're not sending him up for popedom."

"You're playing a dangerous game," Del said. He tilted his hand forward and back. "This *is* important, this *isn't*. What are you going to tell him when he becomes a True Believer? You going to cook fish every Friday?"

Carol shrugged. "It might be nice."

"We've got religion in our blood," Del said. "You don't push booze at the kid of an alcoholic. You've got to trust me here, baby. Remember Suzi's wedding?"

Del's family, on his father's side, all belonged to an evangelical church in Kansas. Korean Baptist, they called themselves. She and Del had gone out there for the wedding and she was amazed at how they'd looked. A century behind the times. Homemade dresses, hair tucked behind the ears. No one had warned her and she'd arrived in a tight black number. She grinned now thinking about it, a little blonde girl among the Korean pioneer women. The wind was picking up and she adjusted Jamey's collar off his cheek as she walked.

When she'd told her mother about the conversation, over coffee at a chic little place in her mother's neighborhood, the older woman had been deliberately nonchalant about the whole thing. "It's a family decision," she said simply.

"He's out of his element," Carol said, her voice getting higher. "He's like a fading king."

Her mother stirred her coffee with a measured hand. Carol could see white around the knuckles of her fingers. "Is it bad today?" she asked, her tone changing abruptly.

"It's fine," her mother assured her with a wave. Then she looked down at her hands and pulled at the digits of one with the other. "Seems like the sort of thing medicine should have fixed by now," she said. "Arthritis may not be the glamour disease for R and D like cancer or those childhood diseases." In disgust she swatted at the air. "There's worse off."

Just when Carol had thought the conversation had dropped, her mother grabbed at her wrist. She told her about a young priest at her church. "He's very discreet," her mother said, and Carol could see a smile appear and disappear from her mother's dried lips. "Requirement of the trade."

Our Lady of Lourdes was a large white stone building set back from the street. She passed through the gate and maneuvered Jamey beyond the thick wooden doors. She'd been in a number of churches in her life and they'd all had the huge thick wooden doors. Del said they were there to give Martin Luther a place to nail his infamous laundry list of protests.

The church was deserted at this hour and in the cavernous room the cold tile beneath her created an echo. The pews fell away from her as she walked toward the sanctuary. There were stained-glass windows bracketing the altar but the sun was weak or in the wrong place in the sky and the colored light trickling in reached barely a third of the way to the floor. She heard a door open to her left and a priest appeared from behind the vestry and moved toward her. He didn't make a sound as he approached, floating under his robes. He was young, Carol thought, about thirty-five or so. Genuinely young for a priest, and she was surprised. With her mother, young could mean anything from twenty to fifty. She'd changed dentists once when hers had revealed that he couldn't remember Kennedy. It was probably going to get harder and harder for her mother, Carol thought, the whole world getting younger.

The priest extended his hand and Carol shook it, hoisting Jamey up a little on her hip. The baby looked at her for a moment and then his eyes closed and his head drooped. She wasn't sure whether or not to wake him.

"Relax," the priest assured her. "There's time."

Indeed, they still had to wait another few minutes for Carol's mother to arrive. Carol busied herself with the diaper bag while the priest looked on and tried to engage her in small talk. This stalled quickly and even the priest looked relieved when Carol's mother entered. "Nancy," he said. "Welcome."

"Father John," Carol's mother said with a sigh. "I couldn't find a cab." It was jarring to Carol to see her mother calling anyone Father, especially the kid in front of her. And even stranger to see her apologizing.

He led them into the offices behind the raised platform and took out a clipboard with a pen tied to it. "I'm always losing these," he said ruefully. "There are some questions," he said, "since your daughter is not a member."

"Fire away," Nancy said, and he did, asking for correct spellings of their names, Del's included, and their address and zip code.

"The father is working?"

"He's a bond trader and couldn't get away."

The priest paused for a moment before he wrote this down and then he asked a few more questions, his hand gradually descending to the bottom of the page. When it reached the bottom, he handed her the form and asked her to confirm the information.

She looked it over. The priest had uneven print, as if he was unused to it. Maybe he wrote in script. Priests ought to write in beautiful, flowing script, she thought; then she thought that sounded too much like her mother.

"You have brought no godparents or guests?" he asked, raising an eyebrow.

"I'm here," Nancy said.

"And you are willing to help these parents in their Christian duties?"

"I am," Nancy said. "Yes, I am."

At this, the priest leaned forward. "This is all very unusual," he said. Nancy agreed. He coughed. "It is contrary to the nature of the celebration to perform this rite in such a . . . manner."

Carol found herself drifting while the priest and her mother negotiated a compromise. She could see stacks of paperwork behind the man's shoulder fluttering as the heater kicked on and off. She could see a coffee mug, a pencil. She nodded dumbly when the priest exacted a promise that she would undergo belated catechetical instruction.

"It would be better," he added, "if your husband were to attend with you."

Carol held back at that, imagining how such a conversation might play out. The priest swallowed hard and for a moment Carol wondered if this was where it was going to end. Then her mother jumped in, promising again to take responsibility for her daughter and her grandson, for all of it, and Carol could see the young priest responding to the older woman's entreaties until finally he rose.

"Very well," he said. "Let's begin."

"Ready when you are," Carol said. Jamey woke when she stood and began grabbing at her shirt. The priest led them all to a small basin directly underneath the western stained-glass window. When they got there the priest told her he'd forgotten something in the office, and Nancy, perhaps fearing a last-minute change of heart, followed him, leaving Carol alone. She stared down at the basin. It looked like a bird-bath but of course she didn't say that; instead, she began unbutton-ing Jamey's jumper. It was cold inside the church and when Jamey was naked he squinted up at her, confused. His arms jerked across his body like he was treading water. He began to cry and Carol tried to shush him by rocking him across her breasts. Nothing doing. She could hear the echoes high on the ceiling.

This time Carol heard the priest's footsteps as he returned. "Your mother will be back in a moment," he called. "She's gone back to the car for the garment . . ." When he saw Jamey in his nakedness, the man jerked his head back, surprised. "Generally we perform the baptism with holy water anointed at the top of the head," the priest said. "We do not, as a rule, dunk the child."

Carol flushed. She watched the priest's eyes narrow with quizzi-cal amusement. "I'm—I'm sorry," she said in a sheepish half-whisper. "I think I had a picture in my mind." Beneath her chin Jamey struggled with his balled fists. "It'll be only a minute."

While she yanked and tugged Jamey back into his jumper, the priest stared downward at the floor. When she was finished, Carol handed him the fussing infant and stepped back to give him room to maneuver. Nancy returned with a woolen blanket, ivory-colored and hand-stitched with an intricate pattern. Her mother must have stitched the clever work some time ago, Carol thought, while her hands were in reprieve.

Carol watched, detached, as the priest navigated a series of prayers and blessings, anointing Jamey lightly while her mother whispered explanations about the oil of catechumens. Finally he looked up and motioned Nancy closer to her daughter. "It is time for the renunciation of sin and the profession of faith," he said. And then, in a louder voice that echoed in the empty church, he began: "Dear parent and god-parent, you have come here to present this child for baptism. By water and the Holy Spirit he is to receive the gift of new life from God, who is love." Carol could feel her mother's hand reach at hers as the two women stood waiting to recite their vows. There were a lot of them and Carol had to bite back an impulse to laugh. Such a strange impulse. It was a nervous tic she'd had since childhood. It often happened when she was anxious—but there was something else too. In the church, with the priest using his best Sunday voice, as she and her mother exchanged "I do's" with the priest's prompts, she could not help but feel that she was getting married again. It didn't feel like comedy, exactly, but what it was resisted being named.

The priest motioned Nancy forward. "It would be more appropri-ate for the godmother to perform this duty," he suggested, and neither woman disagreed, although as Carol watched her mother's slender arms, she hoped that today's arthritis was not particularly bad. From the trembling, she guessed that Jamey might end up getting that dunk-ing after all. Nancy hoisted Jamey from underneath the shoulders and the priest cupped water from his free hand to the boy's skull. "I baptize you in the name of the Father," the priest said. The water rolling down his nose left Jamey sputtering. The priest waited a moment and then dunked his hand again.

"And the Son."

Carol waited, holding her breath. "This is it," she thought.

"And the Holy Spirit."

Jamey was nearly purple now from crying. The priest paused for a moment but then continued. "God the Father of our Lord Jesus Christ has freed you from sin, given you a new birth by water and the Holy Spirit, and welcomed you into His holy people. He now anoints you with the chrism of salvation. As Christ was anointed Priest, Prophet, and King, so may you live always as a member of His body, sharing everlasting life," The priest finished. By now Carol had moved ten feet away, her leg pressed up against one of the pews. She could see the light descending from the stained glass, colored rose and blue, strands of dust floating in the air. It was all washed out by the time it reached the priest's broad shoulders.

When he was finished, the priest took the baby from Nancy's arms, draped the blanket over Jamey's body, and then returned him to Carol. She pressed the wool hard against Jamey's puckered skin and then against the wetted collar of his shirt. By the time she had finished, Jamey was sleeping soundly, exhausted from his ordeal.

The priest completed his blessing and Carol found her lips mumbling "Amen" at the appropriate gaps. When it was over, Nancy hugged the priest and whispered something Carol could not hear. He nodded and looked over at Jamey. "Well, we already know he has the lungs of an angel." Carol apologized but he waved it away. "He is a healthy child."

As the priest walked them down the aisle to the exit, Carol thanked him for his help. "I promise to bring Jamey to Mass with my mother," she said. Then she laughed. "He'll be wearing clothes—so no crying."

"I will hold you to that," the priest said, also with a laugh. "It is an important thing you have done here today. You have shown your son the gateway to life in the Spirit."

"Yes," she thought. "That was certainly something." And if it wasn't exactly what she'd expected, she would just have to make do. Jamey looked different now too, quieter somehow. At the very least, things with her mother were promising to thaw. She waited a moment for the older woman to catch up and then reached for the heavy door. "Allow me," the priest said, and Carol tried to smell him as he brushed past her. He smelled like nothing at all. Perhaps a hint of violets, perhaps not. He exhaled as he pushed the door forward and they all blinked at the light flooding into the church. "*Vitae spiritualis ianua,*" the priest repeated, this time in Latin. Outside, a car alarm was blaring.

And so it was done. That night, as she lay in bed—Del had still not come home although it was almost ten o'clock—Carol thought about the entire situation. It wasn't exactly what she'd had in mind, sure, but life was like that. Disappointments big and small. The whole thing had been good for Jamey, one way or another. She murmured the priest's words, *gateway to life in the Spirit*. But the words didn't warm her. In the clear morning light she had seen where the corners of the church were dusty. Neglected. New World dust, like cotton swabs. No ancient dirt left in the city. Maybe if Del had been there, things might have been different. They could have had the ceremony on a weekend, with more than just her mother there, and a luncheon afterward. They could have met with the priest beforehand, or another priest if they'd preferred. Taken the proper classes. Jamey could have had a proper white gown and studio pictures. They could have done it right. Jamey was fussing in the next room and without even thinking about it she walked to the kitchen and began heating a bottle. Everything was Del's fault. Just another life event turned to ashes in her mouth. She dipped her finger in the milk. Not too hot. Since their wedding, everything had been increasingly difficult. Everything a struggle. Nothing easy enough to suit her or him.

Even Jamey's delivery had been a problem. Del yelled at the nurses and doctors, fearful and bullying, clearly outside of his element. "Can't you see she's in pain?" he'd demanded of a nurse checking dilation. "Get her something." Then a look down at her, a quick smile like they were a team in something. Twelve hours of his bluster. Even the nurses showed signs of the strain. Their goodwill had sheared away in the late hours. "Maybe a little quiet?" someone suggested, and when Del started up again, she asked him to leave for a few minutes. "We'll come find you if anything happens," someone said, shuffling him out the doorway. In the end he'd missed the whole thing, down in the cafeteria sulking. Not that it had mattered at the time, but now there was a gash in the retellings, poor Del's own personal story of himself.

She brought Jamey to her bed and bounced him a little on her knee to wake him up. Just another thing that didn't go perfectly, the fairy tale falling short. Jamey ate enough to warm his belly and then dozed off. She let her own head dip, enjoying the feel of him against her, his tiny fingers working in his sleep, worrying her nightgown.

When she woke up, Del was brushing his teeth. He smiled at her, his mouth rabid with toothpaste. "I didn't want to wake you," he said after he spat. "You guys looked comfortable." He leaned over onto the bed and hugged her and she could feel her body harden against his smothering bigness. She turned away, facing the wall, and lay there until she felt his side of the bed sink with his weight. "I put the baby back in his crib." She felt his fingers play lightly along her shoulder and she had to make a deliberate effort not to flinch. Still, whatever she did or did not do, in a minute his hands retreated and she could hear him push air through his lips. "Is it something old or something new?" She didn't respond. "Something borrowed or something blue?" he finished. After a few more minutes, he turned off his light and pulled hard at the covers. And then again. She grabbed onto a handful and pulled them taut against the mattress. "They don't even reach my legs," he said. "You're wrapped in them." He pulled again. "Get up."

Finally she released the great mound from underneath her body and he sighed again and turned over, careful to leave a moat between their two bodies. "My day was fine, thank you for asking," he whispered.

I don't give a damn about your day," she said, her anger surprising herself. "I don't give a damn for any of it. Buy today, sell tomorrow. Sisyphus in suspenders."

Now he didn't say anything, just lay there with his shoulder rolled over and away from her. They were taking turns, she guessed. "What did I do today?" she asked him. "Take a shot at that one." She lifted her feet out of the bed, kicking at the mass of sheets tangled with her toes. "You don't have the slightest idea what we do around here all day. Do you?" she challenged.

"I suppose not."

"That's right," she said. Then she rubbed her neck. "That's right."

He turned over onto his elbow and stared at her, face open. "So what did you do today?" She could see a smile playing on his mouth and she wanted to scratch it off. "Nothing. The baby cried and slept and I cried and slept."

He nodded. "Fine then."

"He's getting older so I'm getting older," she said. "The whole day is his, none of it's mine anymore. Can you understand that?"

His eyes pulled downward in sympathy. "It's a hard time," he said. "Everyone says it'll get easier."

"Everyone?"

He shrugged. "Did you think about getting some help? Maybe your mother? God knows she'd be dying for the opportunity."

"What's that supposed to mean?" Carol asked.

His arms came up in surrender. "It means what you want it to mean. Goodnight."

In a few seconds she sank back down in the bed. "Would it bother you, my mom helping out?" She tried to keep her voice even.

He considered this. "Didn't pick her to raise our children. I picked you," he said, poking gently at her nightgown with his finger.

He tickled her with his fingertip. She pushed him away. "Seriously," she said.

"Seriously? I wouldn't be thrilled but if you need the help . . ."

"I turned out all right."

For a while he said nothing, and then, "You're amassing troops for a war and you don't even know it."

She thought about this. It did feel like a war.

"Once she starts changing diapers, she's going to think that gives her input into other decisions too. The important ones."

"You think we've got all the answers?" she asked.

"Some of them," he said. "She's going to have that kid baptized while we're out at the movies."

She couldn't help it, her leg jerking outward. For a moment she didn't move, hoping it would pass, but he tilted his face until he could see her eyes. She could tell that he knew. He shook his head deliberately from side to side.

And again she felt it rise up inside of her. "What does it matter to you?" she said. "Can you tell? Could you sense it in the three or four seconds of quality time it took to carry your son to his crib?"

"How could you do it?" he asked. "Was I somehow unclear?"

"You talk about my mother," she said. "Why shouldn't she have some say in the decisions? At least she can pick your baby out of a lineup."

"Without me?" he asked, his voice rising. "Without me?" When he was angry he would enunciate. Tiny drops of spittle across her eyelids and lips.

"You're spitting on me," she said.

"No, honey." His lips and tongue wet and exaggerated. "That's the spirit of Christ you feel." He pushed up onto a shoulder. "Feel that?" he asked, each syllable now drenching. "That's salvation." Then he flung himself back down onto his back.

"Just get out," she said in a small voice.

"This isn't right. This isn't how things get done."

When she didn't move, he pulled the comforter from the foot of the bed and left. She heard him settle into the rocking chair in the nursery. Through the wall she could hear the squeak of the gliders on the floor. She started to cry.

She lay in the darkness for a while and covered her head with a pillow. She didn't want him to hear her. She thought about their honeymoon, dates they'd been on in college. The very smell of him used to carry magical properties for her. She'd cut his undershirts into strips and steal them into her purse. Smell them at her office. She kept waiting for that same feeling to emerge about Jamey. The punch in the gut. Angels and harps. Something. But whatever she'd had for Del had dried up and there wasn't anything to replace it, just a hollowness. Nothing like the weight she was looking for. She'd gone to the library and looked on the Internet, glancing furtively over her shoulder. These days everybody was making her feel like a criminal. She didn't tell her mother. She didn't tell Del. She told nobody the awful truth of her days, the long hours spent locked in eye combat with Jamey waiting for the lightning bolt to descend. "Now, damn it," she'd mutter. "Please." The hours of the baby looking up at her expectantly, some nascent voice alerting him that he was getting robbed. Newborn mothers all over her television set bathed in the Jesus rays, pushing supermarket carts dreamily, humming lullabies as they waited at the bank for the next teller. A whole world of people not to talk to. Something dead inside of her, a nest of ashes.

After a while, she heard Jamey crying and then Del murmur something. She went into the kitchen and pulled a dirty glass from the dishwasher. She let the water cool over her fingers. The crying kept coming. Then she heard swearing and a loud thud. In the nursery Del stood with his head against the wall, plaster powder on the knuckles of his fist. In his crib the baby was still crying. When Del turned to her, his face was blotchy and pained.

"I'm sorry," he said and added, his voice fading out, "Sometimes, I can't . . ." In the room of tiny little furniture he looked as large as a giant.

She went over and put her arm around him. He was trembling, fast as a hummingbird. She took his hand and unclenched it gently. The third finger didn't straighten and when she pulled at it he winced. "Broken," he said. Then he pulled her into him and kissed the top of her head clumsily. She let her fingers splay along the small of his back. They stood for a moment and sometime during all of this the baby had stopped crying. She could hear him sucking on his balled hand, finally content and already asleep. "I'll put up some sheetrock this weekend," Del promised. She pulled tighter against him, her nose flat against his chest. Felt his heat.

"I just want us back," he said, and she nodded.

Behind them, Jamey sucked contently, already dreaming about something else. The mythical animals looked different in the half light, shimmering in and out of focus. Carol looked at the gryphons and the unicorns and in the faded light it was easy enough to see their hooves moving. Del's fist had narrowly missed the forked tail of the dragon and the creature curled away from the damage, disdainful. Across the room, over the crib, Carol could see the phoenix with its wings outstretched, a glory above Jamey's head. She could feel Del's heart begin to slow.

She felt something open in her chest. "Please," she whispered.

The Debt

L. C. Ricardo

The first time they called and asked for her date of birth, Lola said, "No, thank you," and that was the end of it. The second time, she obliged them by saying, "October 12, 1947."

This scandalized Sister Ruth. "That's not your birthday," she said.

"I know," said Lola. "That's why I told her."

"What did she say?"

"She started her speech—the one they all say that sounds like they're reading out loud from a telephone book—and got hung up on one particular long kind of word before she noticed. I think she was embarrassed. Said she'd got the wrong Lola."

Lola leaned back into her pillow, quite pleased with her handiwork.

After the second time being asked for her birth date and declining, she said, "You know, it's their own fault if I dropped out of community college and landed all those debts. They told me before I signed on for the loans that they'd help me out of a pickle if it ever came to it."

"You'll never know what kind of help they'd give to you if you don't own up to them first," said Sister, in her most helpful of airs. "How can they help you with your debt if you don't admit you need it?"

Lola glided over Sister's point with practiced skill. "What'd I want to go to more school for, anyway?"

Sister shrugged.

The third time, Lola told Sister, the gentleman who called didn't even reach Lola, but instead an Erica Campbell.

"And?" asked Sister Ruth.

"This one wasn't going to be fooled," said Lola. "He asked me if I went by any other name. So I told him I was in the hospital and to call back at a better time to ask me such personal questions. I could hear him blushing."

"I don't see the point in avoiding them," Sister Ruth said, persisting. "You're only going to rack up more debt after this last stint."

Lola crossed her arms over her chest to keep the remark from sticking.

"Liberty Solutions," Lola said wryly, lip curled in a cat's smile. "What kind of solution is it for *me*?"

Her eyes circled up to the ceiling with the two cracks arranged in a big letter T. She was now so familiar with them that they had almost become like companions, the kind you sit with in waiting rooms for hours and never speak to but can distinguish by their profiles in a lineup, and know them on the phone from the sound of their ragged breathing.

Lola's eyes then trailed down the wall behind the cloudy steel hospital tray, lingering over the sticky remains of a grape popsicle puddling its corners.

Her grandfather liked to slurp popsicles on his front porch on hot afternoons, swaying in slow rhythm on the rickety swing. He would call out to her through an open window as she dried dishes in the kitchen:

"Lola! Popsicle!"

Grape was his favorite flavor.

Later, she'd find him asleep on the swing in the drowsy sun, the melting, half-eaten treat dribbling through his fingers as they nestled in knitted repose over his belly.

She wondered where he was now. They'd gotten into an argument, he and Lola, and he had gone off on one of his escapades, disappearing for days, like he had in her childhood. It took her exactly three weeks to land back in the hospital. She hadn't heard from him in all that time.

"I botched it up this time around," Lola said. Bitterness edged her voice like glass. "I'll make sure next time is the last."

She was acutely aware of Sister Ruth's silence. The holy-roller nun never failed to sprinkle liberal comments over Lola's monologues, as if they were savages in need of baptism.

Lola stabbed her pointy chin in Sister Ruth's direction. "Well? Don't you got anything to say about that?"

Sister Ruth reclined. Her muscles unraveled. For a moment, panic choked Lola, and she thought Sister must be dead. The nun was old, older even than Lola's grandfather, who was at least fifty-six, and she had been in and out of the hospital as many times as Lola had, and for longer.

Lola swallowed. "You dead?"

The silence persisted.

"No," came the reply at last, "but if you're going to act like you're not worth a farthing, you're certainly not worth talking to."

"The hell's *a fatheen*? Is that some of your stupid Canada talk again?"

Lola hoped to get the ever-ready "I'm not from Canada, I'm British," but Sister held fast and resumed her silence.

They didn't speak again until the nurse with ash-dark hair wheeled in the trolley and announced that it was time for their medication.

"And anyway," Lola said, after throwing her head back and swallowing her pill dry, "if you don't talk to me, it's awful stupid to keep asking to have me put up in a room with you."

Lola spoke to Sister as if their conversation had been left off but a minute before, not more than an hour ago.

Sister Ruth ignored Lola and sipped at her water. She swallowed her pills one at a time.

"All of them now," said the nurse, her cheerfulness a headache. "It's important that you take *all* of your medication."

Sister Ruth liked to neglect a rosy, saucer-shaped pill. It would turn up rattling when they changed the pillowcases or protrude from the soil where the ficus roots grew, in a gray plastic pot on the nearby windowsill.

"There you are, Sister Ruth. That's a good girl." The way the nurse spoke, you wouldn't be surprised if she coaxed the pill down by stroking Sister's throat.

Sister Ruth was squat, with a baby face; she reminded you of one of those porcelain figurines in neat, double hair buns and a lucky-red Manchurian smock with matching trousers—a generic figurine, something a tourist might purchase for pennies from a street vendor in Hong Kong but had a price tag for way over its worth in the local Chinese restaurant.

Sister folded her hands into a tight bulb and proceeded to recite her prayers to the ceiling.

"*Spare, O Lord, one polluted by sins: in faults the foremost, in comparison to all others, and do not enter into judgment with Thy servant, for no one living is justified in Thy sight.*"

"I'm not gonna visit you at no convent," Lola said, trying to climb through the praying woman's words.

"Lights out in ten," said the nurse, as she wheeled away the trolley.

Sister took up her silence like an old habit, and without her roommate's incessant chatter, Lola's ties to the present slackened. She was in two places: the antiseptic hospital room with Sister and the cramped compartment plastered with yellowed maps that had been her classroom in grades six through eight.

Mrs. Parsons, her teacher, wore her black hair plastered to her skull in a helmet. Any child's whimper, any mousy dissent, any disruptive laughter from unruly students ricocheted off her like shrapnel from armor. She made them recite the Lord's Prayer three times a day.

The day after Lola's grandfather went to jail, Mrs. Parsons held Lola back while the other children went out to the scraggly lot that passed for a playground where they ate their lunches.

Guiding Lola to take a seat at the student's desk closest to her own, Mrs. Parsons screwed up her face and said, "Do you understand, Lola, why your guardian is in prison?"

"Yes."

In truth she didn't know. Lola's knowledge of her grandfather was in fact a cloud of rumors and impressions. Liquored-up fights. Crooked loans. Dealings with unsavory characters you could only imagine looked like slouching, shadowed villains inhabiting vintage comic books.

"It's a good thing that you are away from him for a time," Mrs. Parsons continued. "Imagine the influence! A good thing for you to see consequences in action. Your grandfather has greatly wronged humanity. He must pay his debts to society."

Lola stared hard at Mrs. Parsons's folded and bloodless hands.

"Are you listening to me, child? It's important for you to recognize . . ."

The hospital lights cut off. Lola rolled onto her side facing Sister and said to her, "You know, there's no point in looking for God in the ceiling."

That was all they said to each other that night.

At breakfast the following morning, the nurse said to Lola, "Good news, sweetheart. The doctor says you can go tomorrow, as long as you promise to attend outpatient sessions this time."

After the nurse exited the room, Sister felt the need to elaborate. "You know a promise is your solemn word."

Lola smirked—a little too hard, though, because the corners of her mouth smarted.

Lola thought of the silence rattling around in the neglected, empty rooms of her apartment, her time-traveling brain, and the strangling ring of the phone announcing the calls from debt collectors. She thought of the withered leaves of paper with her late college scribbling on them, and nighttimes spent curled up with Ovaltine and insomnia. She thought of all these things, jumbled around like tin cans in a shopping cart.

Then she thought about her grandfather calling her from jail at the foster home two days after her conversation with Mrs. Parsons, telling her she had to testify on his behalf. Telling her she owed it to him for raising her. That had been the first time she hung up the phone on someone collecting a debt.

"I'll think about it, anyhow," Lola said to the nurse, though it was for Sister.

It was not a whole concession, but it seemed to satisfy Sister Ruth. Lola could see a cheerful smile creep up into the nun's eyes.

The direct result of Lola's agreeableness was this: For the rest of the day, Sister pried into Lola's doings and sayings with the precision of a toddler wielding a mallet.

"Oh, it's them again," she said when the nurse approached with the phone for Lola. Her little eyes squinted up in a grin.

"Is this Lola Macintosh?" said the voice.

"Yes."

"Good. May I speak to you for a moment?"

"No," Lola said.

There was a sputtering on the line. "Wh—? Then the—"

"Have a nice day." Lola hung up.

Sister Ruth twittered.

Lola reeled on her. "Next time those Liberty debt collectors call, I'm gonna send them after *you.*"

Sister Ruth closed her eyes, her smile steadfast. "So be it," she said.

Toward evening, Sister Ruth thumbed through the birth-announcements section of a pawed-over newspaper. Sometimes she licked her fingers and moved them as if to turn the page, but then her hand hovered in midair. Lola saw her cast her eyes like a pair of black dice.

"Hey, Sister," she said, "what's caught you up now?"

Sister's eyes slid to her. She put a pudgy finger to her mouth. "Shhh."

Lola summoned a stage sigh, but she fingered for the button that would call the nurses, just in case.

Later, when the ashy-haired nurse rolled in the trolley with their evening meds and her "lights out," Sister bent forward to speak to the unsuspecting woman in confidential tones.

"I know what they're here for. I know what they want."

The nurse fidgeted with the loop of keys at her waist and glanced down at her ugly rubber-soled shoes.

Sister wagged her eyebrows at her knowingly, then took her pills.

"No one's here, Sister. They don't want anything," said the nurse. She was uneasy; she double-checked the medication dosage on her clipboard, bit her lip, and bustled out of the room.

"She forgot to say ten," said Lola, trying to engage Sister.

Her roommate only squinted and muttered.

Lights went out as usual.

During the night, Lola dreamed that Sister Ruth and Mrs. Parsons were both walking on high wires, each holding a pole to balance. Presently, Lola realized that she was on a third high wire, balancing herself on it between the wires of the two women and trying not to fall. She was holding something that was burning, she couldn't tell what. She held out the burning object, wavering in her balance, to Mrs. Parsons, who shook her head. Then Lola held it out to Sister Ruth, who squatted, plump as a pigeon on a telephone line. Sister offered Lola her balancing pole and took the flaming thing from her in return. But it slipped in passing, hitting Sister's wire and setting it on fire. Sister's wire snapped.

Lola woke before she could see the outcome of her dream. It was eleven minutes past two, and she shot out of bed and fumbled to switch on the light, her IV trailing behind her.

Sister Ruth was yelling.

She yelled and yelled, and said, "I didn't take it. Oh, glory! I've had it all along. You'll see. I am the one. Don't tell anyone else. Help! Help! They've come to get me. Or I came to get them, or go to them, or be them. I've got a ladder here, and I know how to climb up and get out. I'll use it to get away. I know they've been waiting."

Night nurses swarmed the room.

One shrill nurse called for the orderly, a black man with round muscles bulging through his green scrubs. He entered, knocking Lola over. She fell hard, putting out her hand to brace herself. Something in her wrist cracked and she shrieked in pain.

An older nurse pulled her up by the elbow with one hand and took Lola's IV drip with the other. She guided Lola from the room with dutiful nudges.

Lola thought her mouth before her first meal in the morning always tasted like a cross between a rotten lemon and sawdust.

That was her first thought upon waking.

Her second thought, after taking stock of her surroundings, was *This is not my room.*

Then she remembered the night before: the doctor examining her wrist, pressing and twisting it so that the pain shot through her until she passed out. She remembered waking to the same pain scrambling her senses like static on a television screen, and straining through it to hear the nurse tell her they were giving her morphine so she could sleep. Telling her she wasn't supposed to get out of bed until the doctor examined her again in the morning. She also remembered catching herself in the nighttime reflection of the hospital window as she threw a dirty look at the hard bundle swaddling her right hand and wrist.

Lola got out of bed and slipped down the hall when no one was looking. The IV glided behind her like some gruesome external organ.

She stuck her head in through the door of her late great room. A very tall and unruffled nun in the chocolate brown of a full Franciscan habit circled, packing away three or four items—the extent of Sister Ruth's belongings.

"Did that Sister *finally* go home?" asked Lola.

The unknown nun turned to Lola, pressing her lips together. "Yes. She did," the nun said with a weak smile.

Lola brought her body after her head into the too-white room. The bedsheets and curtains matched the empty walls, as bleached as the snake's skull the boys used to fawn over in her tenth-grade science class.

"Tell her I'm not coming back next time," Lola said. "Tell her I mean it."

The severe nun shook her head.

Lola licked her lips and shifted her weight. *Don't say anything to me, then*, she thought. *See if I care!*

But the nun held something out to Lola. "Here."

It was a prayer card with lacey edges, a hazy picture of an effeminate Jesus suspended in crucifixion.

"In memory of Sister Ruth. Lola, right? She was always very fond of you."

Lola scoffed. "Thanks a lot."

The nun bobbed her head and left.

"What am I supposed to do with this?" She spoke into the room's whiteness.

Lola turned over the card. Words were printed on the back, small and ugly, like Lola's chicken-scratch.

She held the card above her head so the light coming through the curtains illuminated it. She read the words aloud.

"For those, O Lord, who have not prayers offered for them by another. We lift them up to Thy merciful and bounteous Heart. We ask Thee to bring them into Thy glory and give them a share in Thy Resurrection. For by the Cross our debt is repaid . . ."

The sensation of freezing water prickled along her spine. Her throat constricted. Her gaze fixed upward, Lola lowered the card.

In the ceiling, the two cracks intersected to make the letter T. She imagined they were descending like arms to embrace her. Once more, she was in the classroom with Mrs. Parsons; then in the hospital room with Sister; and finally in the empty, ringing rooms of her apartment with the scattered papers and the sense of decay that had long seized her.

Above these scenes and containing them all was the cross, seared through and scarred into the drywall.

Excess Baggage

Caroline Valencia-Dalisay

"No, ma'am, I did not tie Delilah to a tree," I told Mrs. Figueroa. "Just her bow."

"The bow was attached to her dress," she said in the way that a principal would.

"But I didn't know, Mrs. Fig," I murmured, as if that would diminish my sin or maybe even purge it.

She came around to the front of her desk and sat on the edge. Did I call Delilah *malandi*? she wanted to know. She leaned toward me, smelling of Vicks VapoRub or mothballs, I couldn't tell which, her pores clogged with talcum powder.

"Miss Marquez," she asked again, this time Perry Masonish, "did you call Miss Corpus *malandi*?"

"It wasn't as bad as what she called me, ma'am," I said.

She straightened back up, wiggled her body to realign what had gone askew, crossed her arms under her chest, rolled her eyes inside her head and then hurled them at me punctuating her question. "And what might that have been?" she asked, as I thought she would, even though I knew she knew.

"She called me *anák sa labás*," I said. She looked left, where Jesus was, then right at Mama Mary, as if asking them for comments, but they were silent, as statues would be.

83

"And how, pray tell," she asked, "was that worse than what you called her? You practically called her a harlot!"

"She insulted Mama," I said. "You know what *anák sa labás* is, Mrs. Fig." By calling me a child born out of wedlock, she was aiming for Mama. *Malandi* was exclusively an insult to Delilah. No mamas attached.

"You're only twelve, for heaven's sake," she squeaked. Mrs. Fig squeaked when she got excited. (Actually, she was called "Mrs. Pig" because nobody in the Philippines could pronounce the letter F.) Why they had all those names using letters nobody could pronounce was beyond me. Even "Philippines" came out sounding like "Pilipins."

"Such transgressions at a young age," she said. I knew tying someone to a tree was a bit vicious but I didn't think it was as terminal as she made it sound. I've transgressed. She swayed her head from side to side (piglike) in disbelief at what came out of kids' mouths those days. When she regained her composure, she sighed and delivered the consequences of my bad choice.

"All because Delilah was crowned Muse," she said, lifting her gaze above my head, tilting her head this way and that way as if addressing an audience she imagined was in cahoots with her.

It wasn't that, for heaven's sake. Even though I didn't think she deserved to be Muse. Muse is supposed to go to the prettiest girl who would serve as an inspiration to the class. That was so not Delilah. She probably bought votes, knowing her. But I didn't care. I wouldn't even care if she was crowned Miss Philippines or Miss World or Miss Black Hole. But Lake slow-dancing with her? You don't dance with people you talk smut about. He and I were a team against that snob, that maid-abusing prima donna. (She called her maids morons if they couldn't guess which shoes she wanted to wear with the outfit she picked out for the day. She had so many pairs you would think she had a thousand feet. If she were to die a saint—like that was going to happen—she'd be a patron saint of shoes. She and Imelda Marcos.)

But there was no making Mrs. Fig understand that. Not without telling her that Lake and I conducted marathons of lobbing names at Delilah. And not without getting demerits of all sorts after admitting to such conduct. And not without my telling her I was in love with Lake. And will marry him someday. Never mind that we were not in the same financial status and his parents would never approve of me, but I decided I'm going to be rich someday if it kills me. And never mind that I was only twelve.

I would have let the dance issue pass had Delilah not rubbed things in my face that next morning, laughing an annoying laugh, glancing sideways my way, then to Lake, shielding her mouth as she whispered something to him. That was when I snuck behind her with her back against the tree and I tied her (bow) to a branch. She leaned forward when she felt something tug her from behind but bounced back to the tree, like a suspender plucked from a chest and snapped back. I thought it was funny. Delilah didn't, apparently.

"*Anák sa labás*!" she said, her neck veins straining like squeezed balloons.

"*Malandi*!" I said. After which I had a momentary urge to say the Act of Contrition but then she called me a *anák sa labás* again. I was about to let Mr. Hyde loose from Dr. Jekyll but Lake's glaring eyes pounced on me as if to say 'Enough!'

He eventually got her bow untangled from the branches, between snickering and hushing her, but not fast enough to catch me. The news got to Mrs. Fig quickly. The dance was Saturday night; Sunday, I committed the transgression. Monday, first thing, there I was being sentenced.

"Report in my office after school to apologize to Delilah. Then you are to help Mr. Santos pick up trash around the campus for a week," Mrs. Fig said.

After I collected my jaw from the floor, I said, "I will clean the campus for two weeks and I'll apologize to the superintendent, or the pope, just do not make me apologize to Delilah. Please, Mrs. Fig," I added to show I meant it.

She did the wall-to-wall pendulum with her eyes again and told me I would apologize to Delilah and not to worry, Delilah would apologize to me. After all, she was a fair woman. "Ah, ah, ah," she warned me when I started opening my mouth again. "Enough was enough, young lady." And she dismissed me with a brush of her hand. But she kept on.

She said I ought to be ashamed. She said my impertinence was certainly getting in the way of my becoming valedictorian. (With Delilah's money, as dumb as she was she'd be both valedictorian and salutatorian anyway. And why wouldn't she be after two years as a freshman. And two years as sophomore. It was unlikely my impertinence would be to blame.)

She said that I must think everyone was beneath my level of comprehension, didn't I? And that if I thought my quick-wittedness gave me authority to scorn others in the pretense of brilliance, I had better think again because spitefulness and arrogance could make even the very wise sound very stupid. And moreover, she added, desperate. She puffed out the word: "Dhesphherhat-h!"

And, I would go to confession sooner than Saturday, if she were me. (It was a Mama thing, the weekly confession. Mama said if we thought it necessary to take a daily shower, why on earth would a weekly cleansing of our souls be too much?) The Lord may decide to gather up His harvest before Saturday, Mrs. Fig said.

"And you know where the weeds are thrown," she said.

I did.

"That's right. Gehenna," she hissed. I thought smoke was going to come out her nostrils or other such vents. When she used Bible-sized words like that, I knew it would mean some serious reparations for my sins.

Did she make herself clear? (She punctuated each word with her eyebrows.)

I bounced my head up and down in an emphatic nod and said I was profusely sorry in an effort to reply as big as her question seemed to be.

Then she asked what I was standing around there for, and told me to go on, get to class before I miss out on my academics, which clearly was all I excelled in. She did the brushing with her hand again and turned away.

I was hoping Delilah would forfeit, but when I got to the office after school, she was already there. I could tell. Her stench polluted the air; her perfume could attract flies and gnats like mango peels in a garbage can.

"What's that smell?" I asked.

She called it imported, some extract of something and something. Expensive stuff, she said, I wouldn't know. Some three-letter acronym I bet she couldn't even spell.

I told her I could have bottled rat urine and bat spit and sold it to her for less.

She told me I was just jealous because I couldn't afford perfume.

I told her I wouldn't wear that perfume if I owned the company that sold it.

She called me poor.

I called her worthless.

She said I had no class.

I said she had no IQ.

"You'll never be good enough for Antonio," she said. Her head wobbled. (It would. It was empty.) And she used Lake's real name when talking to me, as if doing so would put distance between me and Lake. As if she was saying "That's Antonio to you."

"Your mother, for crying out loud, a dancer at a club," she said. "Your father, who knew what he really was? Left your mother pregnant," she said shaking her head. "Good thing my uncle saved your mother, no? Wish she hadn't brought him down in status, though."

"Your nose is running," I said. She reached up her nostrils and then had to quickly reach inside her mouth to remove her gum, then tucked it under the windowsill because Mrs. Fig was emerging from the back (looking like she had issues of her own, resting a broom on the wall, her hair in disarray, as if she just arrived from a flight).

Ah, there we both were, Mrs. Fig said. "Let's get this show on the road." And she clapped her hands, then planted them on her hips and said, "Okay." Which was my cue, I supposed.

I closed my eyes and began. "Delilah, I know I humiliated you," I sang. "You screaming like a lunatic like that. And then what was Lake thinking? Tsk! Pulling you up with your bow still fastened, strangling you. Forgive me, Delilah. I made you look like a fool," I said. "And sorry, I practically called you a harlot in public."

Delilah's gills were flapping and after a few powerful inhales and exhales, she tossed her hair and said she forgave me. She said she knew I could not help myself being what I was (up and down stare) but still, she said, she was sorry she had to say it.

There, Mrs. Fig said, now all I needed to do was forgive Delilah.

I would rather slug her, but okay, I thought. "I forgive you."

Mrs. Fig said we'll all feel better about this. "Trust me," she said and told me to run along and go see Mr. Santos in his shop. I obliged without delay but I did remind Delilah of her gum before I ran off.

Mr. Santos was a short, thin man, dark, bent like a lowercase *C,* like he was always crouching out of sight. When I found him, I told him who I was and why I was there and I shook his hand when he extended it. It was coarse. He smiled and said it was a pleasure to meet me and was sorry that it was under such circumstances. I didn't expect him to be so gallant and conversational. He talked as we went around the campus picking up trash. I yes-sirred and no-sirred as appropriate.

"What, sir?" I asked when I realized he had been asking me something.

"What do you want to be when you grow up?" he asked as an adult would, as if an adult must ask that question to make a child feel important.

"I don't know," I said as a child would, as if that would stop the adult from prying.

"Oh," he said, "you must know what you would like to do." How old was I? Eleven? Twelve? Yes? What do I see myself doing in six or seven years?

"I hadn't thought about it," I replied. I asked what he saw himself doing when he was my age. I asked without meaning to be impertinent and told him not to please think me rude, because people who didn't know me thought me so when I asked questions like that. That was how I got myself into trouble sometimes, I said, that and my temper.

He wanted to be a lawyer, he said.

"Oh," I said, "so what happened, sir?"

His parents died young, he said. To make a long story short, he said, he had to quit school and got a job as a groundskeeper and that was all he'd ever done. He said it almost in a whisper, as if he meant to say it only to himself.

"Hmmmm," I said, having nothing to say to rectify his situation.

"I want to be Mrs. Antonio Lacquian Regala," I said.

"Come again?"

"That's what I want to be when I grow up," I said, "to be Lake's wife." I somewhat surprised myself at the trust I placed in him. I hadn't told anyone that before. But, I figured, after all, he confided in me his grave misfortune and it was only fair that I gave him back something as frank and weighty. "But I have to get rich first. Being poor seems to be what makes me lose my battles," I said. "That and being illegitimate. I know there's nothing I can do about being illegitimate, but I'll work my way to wealth so that uppity people will consider me. No, not consider. Pursue," I said.

"Hmmmm," he said. Then, after a respectful pause, he handed me the bag of garbage and said we were done for the night. That disappointed me, thinking I judged wrongly in confiding in him. Until he spoke again.

"God will not give you a snake," he said, "if you ask for a fish."

"I guess the trick would be knowing the difference?" I said, tossing around snakes and fish in my head.

"It would be," he said. "I think they call that discernment," he added, enunciating the word with perfection. I thought to myself that this man missed his calling. He should have been a priest. "Father Santos" does have that sound that clicks in place.

I carried the bag to the receptacle but it was too high, so I had to jump up a little and throw the bag up like one would shoot a layup with a basketball. I missed. The bag hit the rim, cracked open, and its contents spilled on me before hitting the ground. I scanned the area to see if I had an audience. Nobody but a goat. I thought it was Delilah. He came out from behind a tree. It must have escaped from the farm next door. Mr. Santos said not to worry, as he shooed the goat out the gate, and that all I had to do was sweep the trash back into a heap and he'd move it into the bin. I built my pile. It seemed at its foulest when stirred so I let the mountain be.

I said goodnight to Mr. Santos, who thanked me about a million times. You would think I volunteered out of my own benevolence. He offered to fetch me a tricycle to get me home, but I said the walk would do me good, plus I wouldn't want to offend the tricycle driver with my smell. These motorcycle taxis weren't exactly equipped with windows to segregate the driver from the passenger. I'd be in a little cab closely joined to his motorcycle, definitely within his smelling radius. He said to go straight home. I said, "Of course, sir." Where else would I go reeking of garbage like that? So I walked home, ill-scented.

America came to me in an apparition, as it often did at times like those. Disneyland. Ice-cream sundaes. Hershey bars. It was not my fault. I never would have fantasized about America had my parents not insisted on the ridiculous nonsense that we'd be going there someday. "Soon," they'd add. I wished it wasn't such a far-flung idea. The back of our house faced endless fishponds and rice fields beyond which were the blaring lights of Clark Air Base in Angeles City. They seemed enticing and intense but as distant and unreachable as America itself. It didn't matter that Papa had applied for a working visa almost five years ago, and not even a *psssst* from the American embassy. Still, they insisted, we would be going to America. The land where you have every opportunity and absolutely no reason not to get rich unless you were lazy. At least that's what I heard about the place. We were going abroad, they said. Folks in the Philippines said "abroad" as if it was a country. As if it was synonymous with America. They said it roaring their *r*'s as if the emphasis would authenticate it.

But adults, one knows how they are, promise things they never fulfill, my parents included. They'd say things like "One of these days we'll get a new sofa," or "We'll have the radio fixed" or "We're going abroad." That was when I'd get up and find something else to listen to, like the jeeps buzzing by Sunset Boulevard or bamboo stalks rubbing against each other, or our pigs snorting at the air as if asking for deliverance from their own odor.

But I had to have one over Delilah, so I latched on to "abroad." I didn't get why people thought she was pretty anyhow. She was just well dressed, that was all. Even our durocs would look nice in her get-up, or any other kind of pig, for that matter. She was light skinned, yes. That always worked in one's favor, seemed to make up for flaws like dumbness.

"Child," the old folk would say to me, "too bad you're dark. You'd be pretty otherwise." And then another would counter to speak in my favor, saying that at least I was smart. And then another with a simplistic purpose in life would say, smart won't get her a man. They all meant well because after that they'd offer me advice on how to make the best of my good features despite my pigmentation issues. And then they wished their children were as brilliant as I was and wouldn't mind them looking like me. Then they'd ask when are you going abrrrrroad? There might be hope for me there, like getting lighter skin.

I was about a few yards away from the school when I heard someone trailing me. I got a little scared, especially since President Marcos just recently imposed martial law on the city, but it wasn't like I was violating curfew or anything, unless my smell was that offensive. I was irritated more than scared that someone would be tailing me, derailing me from my thoughts. Lake?

I walked faster.

"Lucky, wait, please," he said.

It was.

"What's happening to you?" he asked.

He couldn't figure that out? "You are who you dance with." I walked faster.

"India!" He shouted again.

He rarely called me by my real name. I faced him, my eyebrows overlapping. "Why do you pretend you can't stand her?" I asked and, after a pause, added, "Antonio!"

"You don't have to pretend," I continued. "I never said for you to hate her with me—I can do that on my own."

"Who?" he asked.

"Who!"

He asked if I was mad at him because of Delilah, as if the idea was inconceivable.

"Why am I even having this conversation with you?" I asked. "Didn't we talk smut about Delilah? Don't even try to make me think you didn't."

Why was it all a shock to him that I was angry that he was now chummy with her?

Was I angry at him because of Delilah?

"What do you think?" I asked. I turned from him and started running off.

"Wait!" he said. He wanted to tell me something if I'd stop a minute.

"I don't want to hear it," I yelled back over my shoulder. "How stupid of me to think we were friends. Traitor!" I said. As I ran full speed, I puffed in fumes and for sure he was still watching me, but I knew he was no longer following because I couldn't hear pebbles crackling except for the ones under my own feet. "Why did I even think I wanted to marry him?" I said to myself.

"Would you please stop." He continued to shout, although from a farther distance now. He yelled something about leaving.

I stopped and looked in his direction. "Good riddance!"

Lake had been my neighbor since first grade. He and his parents moved from Manila into his *lolo's* house (more like a palace), the house to our left. I can't say it was the house next door because it was over a hundred yards away. In between us was a vacant lot that we used as a playground. During the rainy season, *carabaos* hung out there after their mud bath in the ditch. So pretty much for the last half of the year, we hung out with these water buffalo. And in the dry season, we flew kites in the lot. Lake said his *lolo* willed the house to his father. His *lolo* was his father's father. Our home was just a humble bungalow; it looked like an outhouse next to theirs. Our backyard was lined with a row of pig-pens housing a handful of breeders. His parents were not too thrilled about the smell. They sent their houseboy, chauffeured, of course, to the municipal building to voice their complaints. Nothing came out of it. Nothing ever did.

When Lake first came out of their palace I was making a basin in the mud and filling it with ditch water. He asked what I was doing.

I told him I was making a pool for my tadpoles, what did he think I was doing?

"What tadpoles?" he asked.

"Ones I'm going to catch," I said.

He asked if he could catch some too.

I said sure but he ought to take off his jacket. What was he doing wearing a heavy jacket like that anyway?

He said he might catch a cold. "It was rainy," he said.

"It's only June. The rainy season has barely started," I said. "The sun is still warm."

"It's all right," he said. His mama did not want him to get dark.

"She ought to make you wear a mask, too, then," I said. "What good are light arms with a dark face?" He was pudgy, smooth skinned, and pale. He must have been sheltered from the sun and mosquitoes and obviously not deprived of extra helpings of rice. He looked worried when he saw the gnawing *carabaos* staring at him. I think he feared they were contemplating their next meal. He flinched when their tails, tassels all tangled in mud, swatted flies on their backs.

"Phhhh. They're just *carabaos*. Haven't you seen *carabaos* before? You aren't afraid, are you?" I asked.

He said, "Why would I be?"

I said, "Good! Because we're going to ride them later." And I told him to pick the one he wanted. I didn't think he could turn any whiter.

"Put your palms together and open them like a bowl," I told him.

"Huh?"

"I thought you wanted to catch tadpoles," I said.

He did, he said, and took off his jacket. I looked at the nearly alabaster skin and said to myself, "And I thought his face was pale!"

"Lower your hands slowly into the water like this." I showed him. And as he lowered his cupped palms into the muddy water, he yelped at first and then started giggling at the tadpoles squirming and twitching, the water draining from his palms as he brought them up. Just then his *yaya* (I had never seen a nanny looking so . . . prosperous) came out screaming.

"Antonio Lacquian Regala! Get in the house at once! If your mother finds out about this, she'll have my throat!" she yelled.

Lake slopped the tadpoles into the pool but one got caught between his fingers. I told his *yaya* it was my fault and not to scold him. She looked at me like I was not even fit to address her, grabbed Lake by the hand, and hauled him home. Halfway down the road I heard her scream. She must have found the tadpole.

Lake waited until she was away at market and then he came out with a china cup. In it was the stiff tadpole in its watery grave.

"Thank you," he said.

I squinted at him.

"For sticking up for me," he said. He said I was his best friend and then asked me what my name was.

"India."

He crinkled his nose and asked if it was a nickname.

I glared at him.

"Well, do you have a nickname?" He did, he said, "Lake."

"Interesting," I said. "You have a mouthful of names and it came down to that."

"Best friends have pacts," he said. We had to have one. He tried out a few on me, tapping me on the head or shoulder or spitting. I told him to stop or he'd be swimming with the deceased.

He kept on, but to himself. And then landed on one he was most proud of. "This one," he said. He held his right hand up like he was pledging allegiance, then folded it and tapped it on his heart. "Now you," he said.

"Phhh!" I said. Then we both saw their car coming up the street.

"I won't leave until you do it," he said. So I did.

His *yaya's* snout stuck out the window and she started screaming his name. He said he had to go. Then he turned to me and smiled. He's had my heart ever since.

It didn't take long before he started acting and looking like a native, climbing coconut trees, swimming in the river, racing *carabaos*, shoeless, shirtless. He was looked upon as a leader among our group of friends because he was rich doing common-people tricks. Often, when we were out and about gallivanting, he would stop at a store and get himself a snack with a couple of extras to go around. I thought it was too much of an imposition and scolded the gang to stop taking advantage. I always refused when he offered me a coke or something, but by the third urging I'd surrender.

"Why do I intimidate you?" he asked once, wrapping his arm around my neck, pretending to choke me, his watch on my face.

"You wear that big Timex, for starters," I said.

"Get off your *carabao*," he said, and then put his Timex on me. I was only ten then; I'd consider myself betrothed otherwise. Besides,

Papa made me give it back.

His skin had darkened to a caramel, then gradually to cocoa. His parents threatened to lock him up in his bedroom if he got any darker (as if that was possible. To get any darker, I mean). Or worse, they'd move back to Manila. If they caught him one more time with those filthy beasts, for sure they'd be packing their bags back to Manila. I hoped by "beasts" they meant the *carabaos*. He didn't take their threats seriously because somehow he knew there was too much risk for them in Manila. Mr. Regala was involved in politics and he was told to resign from his position if he would not go along with what was being asked of him. So he resigned. That was how they came to San Isidro. I already heard it from the town gossips, but I feigned innocence when Lake told me.

"We're not going back," Lake said. They bought property in San Isidro practically as soon as they unpacked their bags. People were spreading rumors that Mr. Regala was paid a good sum by the government to keep quiet. And as if Lake knew what I was thinking, he said, "They made him resign; they had to give him money to compensate for his loss." Then he quickly rescinded what he just said, thinking he ought to hold back. I didn't pry. We all had demons, and I was not an exorcist. He was convinced they were permanent residents of San Isidro. And that was good enough for me. But he still jumped off the *carabao's* back as soon as he saw his parents' car coming. I was so afraid that they would send him back. What was I to do then?

"Oh, let him go back to Manila," I said as I entered my house.

"Who are you talking to?" Papa asked. Lost in my thoughts, I didn't realize I was already home.

"No one, Papa," I said. And I took his hand and pressed the back of it to my forehead; then I released it so he could make his sign of the cross on me with it. I waited for his customary blessing but instead he said that I had better go inside and wash up.

I said, "Yes, Papa." And I threw myself into the shower.

I heard him say he hoped I paused for the Angelus—or did I even hear the bells? he wondered.

I didn't hear the bells.

I heard Papa say "What am I going to do with you, missing the Angelus, tying people to trees and calling people names?" He shook his head, I was sure, as he often did, when he was in disbelief at what I had done. In the midst of his complaints, he was fixing my dinner.

Ever since they told me I was not Papa's, I watched out for signs of resentment, but I couldn't detect any. I thought he was more careful about how he talked to me post-revelation. I wouldn't have guessed the truth if they hadn't told me. Papa loved me more than life and I felt the same about him and Mama. I had just turned seven when they told me. I guess that was the age I was deemed old enough to understand.

"Sit down, India," was how Papa started. The hand on the switch, as it were. I remembered it was a beautiful night lit with fireflies. And on that beautiful night, my identity was dimmed—lost amid the confusion of lights.

Thomas Napoli, my biological father, died before I was born. He was a missionary. He met Mama in a restaurant in Angeles City. Mama, because her family was poor, had to help make a living and that was what she was doing: waitressing. Contrary to Delilah's version, Mama was not a dancer. Not a caged dancer, not a topless dancer, not a pole dancer. Not a dancer, period. She and Thomas had frequent secret meetings and were to elope one night, but he was called to go to India (hence my name; glad it wasn't Turkey—I would have been Turkey Napoli? God does work in mysterious ways. When I told Lake that, he said I was lucky, hence, his nickname for me—Lucky). Thomas wrote Mama a note with a vow to take her away when he returned from his assignment. But he never made it back. He and the other missionaries in his group were killed by Antichrists. "So they said," as Delilah would put it.

Mama in the meantime was pregnant with me and she had to hide her condition because her parents would kill her if they found out. It might have been meant figuratively, but it could have been our tragic communal death had she not escaped. Mama ended up in San Isidro, where she began looking for a family that needed a nanny. It was Papa's family. He, his sister, his sister's husband, and their two-year-old fiend (who I would come to know only too well), and Papa's parents, the whole pack.

Papa was smitten at first sight and knew Mama was the one he wanted to marry. His family did not approve of Mama because of what she was, hired help and pregnant at that. They got married in a church when I was two. Just the three of us, with Father Rey and a couple of witnesses Father Rey grabbed from the streets.

Mama almost died giving birth to me "due to complications" so she couldn't have any more children, they told me. That was one reason they put off marriage, because they waited for Mama to recuperate.

"But why didn't you get married before I was born, if Papa was so smitten?" I asked. "Because," Papa said, "Mama said no to me the first time and the second time as well." I turned to Mama for an explanation. She said she wanted to make sure Papa was sure. But she saw how he was with me when I was born. So she knew she had to say yes at Papa's third try. They both got teary-eyed at the telling of their own fairy tale.

After they got married, Mama and Papa moved out of the mansion and got a smaller house, squandering a portion of his allotted inheritance. He was taken out of the will after that. Mama and Papa loved each other. But to his family, Mama was nothing more than a gold digger. Mama vowed that she would have married Papa if he had been the houseboy in that mansion. Papa said he would have married Mama if she had been the queen. I would have stuck with the traditional for-richer-for-poorer version. But that worked, too.

Papa didn't put up a fight for his share of the inheritance, so he had to make a living like a normal person. He was an inexperienced accountant but because he had enough rich connections through his father, he found a job in that field anyway. The salary was not enough for him to live the way he was accustomed to, but going back home was not an option, so he applied for an American visa. That was how we ended up with our bizarre plans for going abroad.

Papa adopted me soon after they got married. Mama said I had always been his child, adopted or not. Papa's eyes got misty again when Mama said that. I should have been moved as well, but I couldn't help thinking of Thomas Napoli. Would he have loved me like Papa? Would I trade Papa for him if he were to show up now? Or at least, share my love between the two? I hadn't yet known about Mr. Santos's fish-and-snake scenario, so I didn't know squat about discernment. But I had always wondered which man had Mama's heart, really.

"I guess you heard our neighbors are leaving," Mama said. I had just gotten out of the shower and she was in my room patting my pillows and straightening out the bumps on my bed, whether or not they needed it.

"He hasn't actually been neighborly of late," I said, "so he can go to the moon if he wants and it wouldn't matter to me one bit." Mama went on to crease the pleats on my drapes. She did that when she was worried. She fiddled a little more with my drapes and then closed out the world.

"Mr. Regala's colleague in Manila is missing," she said. "And there were rumors that he was next in line. No one was sure if it was a threat by the guerrillas or the government. They weren't saying. But they're leaving for safety; they didn't say where to."

One had to be careful in those days of political discomfort; it was impossible really to trust anyone, so it was best to be neutral or at least speak softly when talking about a missing politician or a missing anybody for that matter. So Mama, in case there were spies lurking, spoke in a low voice behind closed drapes and jalousies.

"Lake didn't tell you?" she asked.

"I might have discouraged him a bit," I said. She resumed with her pleating. Then out of the blue, she said, "Papa got his notice from the American Embassy."

I turned around and let my wet hair drip as I processed the news.

She clapped and shuffled and put her hands to her mouth to contain her delight out of respect for the Regalas' misfortunes. Papa came in with a smile (which would have come with a twirl in normal circumstances) and said his interview was in a couple of weeks; then he'd get his visa. He'd leave for America, work on an affidavit of support, then petition us in a year. So come next year around this time, he said, we'd be meeting him in San Francisco.

I pretended to be happy. I went out to see Lake the next morning to tell him, but he and his family were already gone.

"I know you'll miss him," Mama said. Just pray for their safety, she said. Our lunch table won't be the same, she knew, but I had other friends. This comment was meant to comfort her more than me.

"He had been eating at the rich kids' table anyway," I wanted to say. But I kept it to myself. I told Mama that yes, they will be in my prayers. Lake was in my nightly litany anyway. God, please make Lake fall in love with me. Something along that line. She somehow took pride in my association with Lake. I guess he was a trophy. I didn't tell her that I might have lost him awhile back already. He did eat at my table once upon a time, though. If I were to guess why, I'd say he had lost track of his worth between *carabao* riding and tadpoling. But he had since sensed he was out of place. He even started buying his lunch from the school canteen, which the rich kids did. Or if they brought their lunch, it would be wrapped in aluminum foil. We unwealthy kids had ours wrapped in banana leaves.

She could perhaps buy aluminum foil for my lunch, Mama said. I guessed I had thought out loud.

Yes, of course, anything to keep up with the rich kids, I wanted to say. But I said, "No need." And she said she was just saying once in a while, we could try. I said no, I liked banana leaves; they made my rice taste good. She pleated the next panel over.

"I know you mean well, Mama," I said. "But don't fight my battles for me," I wanted to say. "Don't worry about me," I said instead. "Besides, Lake will be back."

A year, four months, and fifteen days later, there I was at Manila International Airport—"MIA," the city people called it—Mama and I were to join Papa. Mama was looking upgraded. Never mind that underneath her painted toes were dead nails, and rubbing against her nylons were her calluses and cracked heels, thanks to her piggery business, which kept her rough and rugged. Her chin was slightly elevated. My classmates and a handful of our friends and neighbors came to see us off. They were duly impressed. Delilah was there, too. She just had to come to make sure I really got on the plane, like going to my funeral to make sure I was really in the coffin.

I wore a blue suit, tailored especially for the occasion, checking it now and then in case it had been soiled or creased or in any way deprived of its crispness. I gave it a brushing with the back of my fingers to flick off imagined dirt. I fluffed my jacket (like one would a bedsheet) so Delilah would get a whiff of the brand-new scent I was wearing. Mother, too, was suited nicely, in a double-knit pink sleeveless blouse, bell-bottom pants, a matching blazer. She was gorgeous. No wonder Papa fell in love with her even if she came with excess baggage.

"We have to go," Mama said. "They called our names."

Suddenly it hit me that I might not be seeing my friends for a long time, possibly for a whole lifetime. Before now I kept myself busy with preparations for the move. Only now did I realize I'd be missing my own graduation, weddings, baptisms. I'd be proxied as maid of honor. I would be an absentee godmother. The first episode of my life was ending right then and I made no attempt to divinize it. Then I saw someone running in our direction. It was Lake. But the crowd was just too thick. He couldn't get through and the guards wouldn't let anyone without a passport beyond a certain point. I hoped I did not imagine the way he looked at me. He smiled, lines appearing at the sides of his mouth, as if he meant to say something parenthetical. I halted and must have stayed still for a while, people bumping my shoulders as they moved toward the gate.

I have to go, I mimed.

Write? He pantomimed.

I nodded.

"You'll see him again," Mama said. I wanted reassurance that America would be merely on probation. But when we went behind the glass walls of MIA, the closed doors muted my previous life with a deafening sound of permanence. My heart stopped.

America was cold. The air was damp. It was eight o'clock at night in August and it was still light outside. It was daylight savings time, they said. I thought it was great that they could save daylight in America.

Papa's flat in San Francisco was nestled in a string of flats that weren't as flat as the word suggested. They were long, narrow buildings that looked from the outside like facades, lifeless. Papa's flat was carpeted, bathtubbed, and fireplaced. Streetcars, not *carabaos*, crossed the roads. Streetlights illumined the night, not fireflies. I ached for home.

I told Lake all that in my letter. I told him it was tough to sleep in a foreign country. But the toughest part was waking up in it the next morning. I told him about school, that America had two extra years before high school called middle school, which meant that the two years I spent at San Isidro High were considered my middle school years and so I was now just a freshman. I wrote this last sentence with multiple exclamation points.

"Don't ask me if they're two years, smarter here," I wrote. "It's just America's desperate idea to segregate hormones."

I clucked all the way out the door of the counselor's office at Kennedy High, where Papa enrolled me and where finally Papa said he had to put his foot down (something he learned in America) and this was what it was going to be. It wasn't like I was demoted, he said. I was just placed among everybody else. He said I should be thankful I was in America now. Half of San Isidro would trade places with me in an instant. What more could I want?

But he cut short his sermon because I think he knew that it wasn't a matter of wanting more, but more of wanting what I used to have. Which was enough.

Lake wrote back saying it was too bad, he'd be in college long before I would get out of high school. It would be great if he followed it up with what problem that would pose, but as usual, he stopped there. He did ask how I was, and hoped all was well. All that bogus stuff. He thanked me for the pictures and said that America agreed with me, it seemed. He bet boys at school were fighting over me. He said not to fall in love too quickly. And then he said some things about the weather and such trivialities. I really wanted to hear what he was going to say that night they were leaving San Isidro and that day I left for America. We were best friends, he said instead, his remark nestled within more weather nonsense. We're best friends and we can tell each other anything, he said.

Sure, we were. We had one of those tight friendships that would never amount to anything. But I didn't say that. A year's worth of letters going back and forth, feeling each other out about whether we were talking about the same thing. And we couldn't talk about his family because it was still politically unsafe. But other news would always push things to the side. Such as the passing of Mr. Santos. The next handful of letters were dirges and salutes to him. The little bent man. His fish and snakes still juggled in my head. I wanted to ask him so badly how I would discern discernment, and panicked at the thought that he would never be able to tell me now. After that my letters were a sundry of complaints about America, how racist, how wasteful, how sinful. Why couldn't Americans be like Mr. Santos? I wrote about my parents, how hard they worked as foreigners to gain half as much respect due them. Papa a bank clerk, Mama a convalescent caregiver. They were just Social Security numbers, green-card holders, always reminded that they were foreigners. They were set in their Filipino ways, their tongues rigid and unable to pronounce words correctly. I was deemed unintelligent, slow to grasp concepts, so everyone talked to me slowly that I might understand. I understood them; they didn't understand me. That was their problem. He wrote back saying he didn't think in his wildest dreams that I would have difficulty with the language. I didn't think I had an accent.

He told me his plans. He was going to take up law. And Delilah, he said, was also pursuing a career in law, he heard. How did I like that? You just never know. How about me? he asked. Did it seem like I was getting where I wanted to be?

I said I didn't know. One thing I did know, though, I told him in a letter, my illegitimacy was not an impediment anymore. I was not condemned for it here. They do not make it their business. Back home we were each other's business whether or not we asked for it. But as far as getting where I wanted to be? You tell me, I said.

I ripped up that letter. In fact, I never wrote to him again. His letters got scarce. Then they became extinct. One year of letters beating around the bush, or maybe not beating around the bush. One year was just too long to leave things unadmitted.

If I heard news about San Isidro, it would be through other friends' letters, which were waning fast as well. Or from people we knew from the Philippines passing through San Francisco on a tourist visa. These old friends and distant relatives would say they'd give our hellos when they returned to San Isidro, but they never did because they never returned home. Somehow they found ways to stay in America. Like falling in love, or so they would say. Through these (permanent) tourists I heard that Mr. Regala was taken prisoner but had been released; the family went back to San Isidro. Lake had to stop college for a while to help run the family businesses but had gone back when his father came back. He wasn't a lawyer, no. He was an agriculturist. I guess you just never know. One of these days, I'd write him again, I told myself. Until one day, it was suddenly seven years later. I received an airmail envelope. I wished life would stand still for one minute in America so I could feel myself move. But it does not wait for one to pause. And before you know it, Lakes are marrying Delilahs.

Their wedding invitation smelled like Delilah, an extract of something and something.

"Are you sure you want to go?" Mama asked.

I asked, "Why wouldn't I? He was my best friend once, wasn't he?" She said she'd go but Papa and she had just renovated the kitchen. They were drained both physically and financially, so it was bad timing. It was great timing, I thought. I wouldn't want Mama to pleat my skirt.

A favor of a reply was requested. I fumbled for a pen and marked my reply, "Able to attend, party of one."

The wedding was a feast of past things, of things almost forgotten, of things I hadn't noticed then but did now. Cousins emerged from everywhere.

"Do you still know little Mila?" someone asked.

"She was only a baby when you left, wasn't she? She's now a teacher," another said.

What about me, what was I?

"A computer programmer . . . Yes, I do like it. It has its perks . . . Yes, good money . . . Oh, how lovely Junior's kids are! . . . Yes, yes, come the right time, I shall have my own replicas as well . . . No, nothing serious yet . . . Just good friends . . . Yes, American," I said, even though I knew by that question they mean, "Is he white?" He was a potpourri of races, really, but I couldn't say that without going over his pedigree and risking acceptability. Not that he mattered that much, I just didn't want to get unnecessarily defensive.

They said I'd changed.

How? I wondered.

They said I looked American. I didn't know what that would be. Americans were an assortment of breeds. I said, I felt the same.

They said I spoke with an accent. It seemed I could not win with that. I struggled to lose one to gain another? I didn't tell them, but I thought they spoke funny. Kind of sing-songy. I noticed their peculiar mannerisms, what with their carrying fans that they waved in front of their faces and handkerchiefs they dabbed on their noses or foreheads to wipe off sweat. It reminded me of Mrs. Yap, my second-grade teacher. She had us pin handkerchiefs on our chests so that we were snot-prepared.

"How is Mrs. Yap?" I asked.

They said she moved with her son into Quezon City since Mr. Yap's passing.

"Oh, it's good to have a son like that," I said. "In America, a good son like that would be checking her into a good home."

Mrs. Fig came up to me. I didn't think she could get any older. Her hair was silver and thin. She said, "It's wonderful to see you again."

She recalled memories of my mischief and then laughed. But how sophisticated I was now! Who would have guessed, I was such a menace back then. I kept the faith, she hoped.

I assured her it was intact.

She said she worried just a tad, because I was quite a piece of work. She covered her mouth each time she laughed and she tapped me on the shoulder for every punch line.

Old friends said their hellos and offered unceasing invitations to have dinner at their homes. I said, "Of course, of course! I wouldn't miss it." Mrs. Fig, too, insisted to be first. And I said, "Yes, I'd be delighted!"

"Beautiful, beautiful," she said.

"No kidding," I said.

Then my heart resumed its beating from that departure day at MIA.

Standing in a white barong was Lake, more beautiful than any groom or bride could ever be.

The wedding was a blur. It was either muffled by the packed church or I'd fainted. Next thing I saw, they were marching out as man and wife. Lake's head slightly turned my way and pointed with his snout to Delilah's bow on the back of her dress. I spat out a laugh and so did he. Delilah looked to where he was looking and saw me. She smiled and waved. I returned the gesture. Didn't we talk smut about Delilah?

At the ceremony, I danced with Lake. It wasn't exclusive. I got in line for the money dance. I pinned my bills on his lapel. He said he missed me. It was nice to see me again. He asked why I was crying. I asked whether he was really that heartless. He said there I go again, the same as before, always making him think there was something he was missing. I walked away as the next person cut in. I made my escape through the back door, but I heard footsteps. I told him to go away.

"What was I supposed to do?" he asked.

"About what?" I said.

"About you and me. You wouldn't write to me."

"What made you think I'm crying about you and me?" I asked.

"So now you're going to make me look like a fool for making something out of nothing?" he asked.

"If you are happy, I am happy."

"That is *carabaos* manure," he said. "I loved you."

"So why did you stop?"

"You wouldn't let me," he said.

"Would she be okay with it if she knew she's second choice?"

"Not second. Better. And I've never stopped," he said.

"Yeah, well, you've made your choice. Oh, excuse me, your 'better' choice." We fell quiet for a while as people passed by and cast their suspicious glances at us. He gave them his smile that would melt anybody's heart—not only mine. He turned to me and said Delilah was his choice because she loved him.

"Lake?" Delilah called. She was radiant, though I hated to admit it. I gave her a hug and she hugged me back tight. I thought I felt firmness on her rounded belly. She said she hoped whatever it was we had in the past would remain in the past and now she hoped we could be friends, knowing that best friends is out of the question as she knew that belonged to someone else.

"How far along?" I asked.

"It was five," she said.

I waited for clarification but when none came, I looked at Lake.

"We lost the baby," he said.

"We were going to name her India," she said.

"I'm sorry, Delilah," I said. "I didn't know." Lake and I exchanged our looks that always meant something that is never said.

"The next one's going to be India too," I said.

"Girl or boy, India it is," she said with a nod.

The glasses were tinkling inside, so I told them they'd better tend to their guests and gave my congratulations again. The maid of honor came out and snatched them up. Lake looked back. I held up my hand and folded it and tapped it on my heart. He would have, if he had a free hand.

I packed for home after feasting daily with friends and relatives for the duration of my visit. It was effortless since I gave away most of my belongings. Nice shirt. Nice shoes. Like your lipstick. I could always get another, I said. They craved American materials, so why deny them if I could comply without sacrifice? I left them all my excess baggage.

The Morning Star

S. L. Scott

I do miss him. When the choirs fill the heavens with voices of ethereal harmony, I sometimes close my eyes and pretend his voice is still among them. His was the most beautiful, with a softness and compassion that warmed the heart and made you long for more when the song ended. Each time I would look upon him and ask, *Just one more, Lucifer,* he'd smile that tender, graceful smile and answer, *Whatever pleases you, my Lord.* And the choir would sing again with my precious angel shining the brightest.

Heaven's beauty has never been the same since I gave him up. But I suppose that's not the right way to say it. Sacrificing my most beloved angel was the most painful thing I have ever done. Perhaps it is because I cannot show my love to him any longer. Humans cannot honor him, nor cherish that once gentle being in which I saw such perfection. They do not understand how deeply I long to reach out and take his face in my hands and whisper *I still love you, my angel.* I cannot allow them this understanding, and it hurts to feel their hatred of him.

Or perhaps it pains me so because his love for me was lost the day I cast him into Hell. I permitted that contempt he felt, the disgust and envy of my throne that sent the heavens crying out in war. I had to do it, yes, I know this. Though the human world was but a glimmer in my plan, there were things that had to be done. My angels—my precious angels—I wanted to give them a purpose. To guide, teach, and protect the creations beneath them . . . to cherish and love them, as I did my angels.

But there was one problem. For humans to possess free will, to give them a choice, any choice, there must be more than one option for them to contemplate. My angels knew only me and my grace; there was no need for free will in them. But the humans, who would one day be bearing the burden of free will, required that I provide them not only with my grace and love, but also with another's. By my own law there could not be two gods, but without a different path, there would be no free will in mankind. It saddened me to make the decision I ultimately did.

In the angelic ranks, there were a few who could handle such a task, but none as strongly as my beloved Lucifer. If I were to give up one whose grace and wonder so filled the heavens with joy. . . if I were to taint that perfect beauty with visions of envy and cast him out of Paradise forever . . . only one God would remain, while humanity would be given the choices needed for free will. No other angel was worthy to become nearly my opposite, and even though it would take him from me for all eternity, even my dear Lucifer deserved a purpose. And for an angel so great, only the most important duty could be given to him.

So, slowly, that pure love was infected till his eyes burned with contempt and his voice rang bitterness throughout Paradise. Other angels, weaker than my Lucifer and long since influenced by his radiance, felt the disgust sink into them until the heavens split. Most of my beautiful angels remained in my glory, bathed with light and cleansed of his sickness. The rest, shadowed in his ravaged beauty, revolted against me.

I could not fight that battle, not until the end when all my angels' hopes had fallen dry and loathing rained in my ruined Paradise. Then, amid the weary bodies, I walked and cleared the darkness from the loyal, and into the shadows ran those chosen to fail me, save one: my glorious Lucifer, as proud and strong standing against me as he was once humble and cherished at my side. Into my arms I took him, a last loving embrace, and upon his brow I placed a chaste kiss. A final good-bye to my angel.

He does not understand the reasons I have done this. I have denied him such knowledge. So true was his love for me, and mine for him, that should he not feel that hate consuming his heart, my angel would return with repentant tears, and I would not dare to stain such purity again. Thus I watch him, playing with unknown piety the role I assigned him. No other could weave such evil, for none, save myself, were so pure in grace and love.

When my garden was created and my angels, both loyal and fallen, began to learn their purpose, dearest Lucifer surpassed them all. With shrewd planning he tempted the woman, sliding in the serpent's body over her bare shoulders to coil around her neck and hold her in false security. His split tongue hissed lies to please and tantalize a child that could not understand what was being offered until she took that fated bite and inherited the awareness that even her mate lacked. Such wonders awareness can bring, though knowledge and understanding do not come so easily with it. My Lucifer knew this and without teaching his ignorant charge what to do with this awareness, he fled from me, but not before taking a moment to whisper a song in the air and indulge in the memory of a paradise lost.

I have watched him many times in the blistering fires of the damned. Far from his brimstone throne, my Lucifer walks among the sinners he created. Their screams abuse his tender ears until some pity returns to his eyes and, for a moment, Heaven's light warms those poor souls he looks upon. But when he returns to the evil that infects him, such scorn he then holds for those most blasphemous of Hell's power that he takes the whip from a lower demon and tears into the sinners himself. When his fury has finally been quelled and blood bathes that which was once pure to me, he walks to the deepest fires and stands with his face lifted to Heaven. I hear his tortured weeping as he stares up at me, the eternal flames burning away his love until only the hatred remains and the cries of sorrow change to screams of contempt that fill Hell with his rage.

He calls to me still, with challenges and cynical damning. He plays with humans and tests them against me, and I allow it. I sacrificed him to give mankind choice, and they are free to be swayed by him and the fallen or guided by my grace and loyal angels. In the end, he returns to his domain consumed by even more hatred than when he came to me, and I find Heaven all the brighter for having seen my precious angel once again. I know I will never hear that sweet voice speak kindly of me again, so I will gladly bear his worship of hatred. As long as my creation abides in him, so does my love.

Intensive Care

Kaye Park Hinckley

At the end of September in northern Alabama, you can't see the end of the road and besides, you distance yourself from any ending. You drive over the top of a swollen hill, between cut-away mountains of changing colors, then down, nudged by a memory of green-tipped beginnings brittled over, now, with too many shades of bronze. On Interstate 65, the white lines slip underneath the wheels and you think you're getting somewhere until the road flattens out. You pass a familiar field of cotton, puffed and split to browning, too late for picking. A man in a straw hat kneels in the middle of a thousand dead white eyes as if what he expected is not what he got.

No more predictable landmarks, only painted lines. You follow them until it's Joe's turn to drive. Without words, you stop somewhere along the road and change places. Then you take out your notebook, but can't begin to write because you don't know the ending. You don't know what will happen to your beloved Jenny, and you don't know who Joe is anymore.

You turn around to watch Jenny sleeping in the backseat, curled up on a pillow: an embryo waiting for birth; a beautiful child, with an appalling tumor taking over her brain. You imagine yourself pulling it off, a ravenous, jellyfish-like thing with the face of a woman you hate. But it holds on with nasty tentacles. Finally, Joe helps you. Together, you and Joe yank it away and throw it onto some beach, where he crushes it with the heel of his polished black shoe. And when Joe finishes off the thing, like Joe should do, the three of you—mother, father, and child—live happily ever after, as if the tumor never took hold of Jenny, as if another woman never sucked the life from your marriage. That's the ending you want, but it may not happen. So you tuck away your notebook. You don't speak to Joe. You keep your distance.

Jenny doesn't wake until Joe turns off the ignition in the fourth level of the hospital parking garage. In the corridors, she smiles at the nurses who welcome her back, a characteristic smile in which her eyes squint up to nothing. "The third time's a charm," one of them tells her.

On the seventh floor, Jenny lies in the bed while the nurse takes her vitals. Joe watches TV. You won't unpack the things you've brought for yourself and Jenny—not yet. Tomorrow, after surgery, you'll be in a different room. You'll be in intensive care, where you will be allowed to stay because Jenny is only six. You know the steps, but you don't know where they lead. If the nurse is right, this time the thing will be scraped away forever. You distance yourself from all but that thought. You pace out the hours left before surgery, hoping they'll hurry before it's too late.

Jenny's nurse comes, a man in a mask. His face will change when night comes. It always does. "Surgery will last for three hours," he says. "You can wait in this room."

No, you can't wait in this room. Not with Joe, anyway. You can't look in his eyes and see the woman's face. He doesn't ask where you're going. You wish he would. You wish he would blink it all away—the tumor, the woman, the last two years. It will never happen again, he said, but you can't forgive him. You aren't God, after all.

The polished floor of the hall shines in front of you, stealing your blurred shape, capturing your footsteps. The entrance to the hall looks exactly like the exit. If it weren't for the numbers on the doors, you could lose your way. In this place, beginnings and endings occur in the same split second. Faces and pain come and go.

You've circled back to Joe. He sits slumped in a brown leather chair. The TV is too loud. You turn it down. He turns it off. You sit face-to-face in silence.

Joe goes to the window. The hours pass, and their passing reminds you: Night hours are slow when you lie alone, when you swing between worry about Jenny and anger about Joe. You go over it again and again, what Joe said when he left. He'd be home by ten from a social meeting with corporate. You trusted him, at first. He said what he meant. He was climbing the ladder of missed meals and late lunches and too many after-hours telephone calls, but he had to play the game. Except that Jenny is his child. She needed him. You needed him, too.

When he finally got home, at dawn, you questioned him. "Why are you so late? Who were you with?" He shouted, "Just leave me alone!" He left to sleep in the den, down the hall from Jenny, whose headaches had started again.

The next morning you mentioned the headaches to Joe. He snapped that you were overreacting as usual. After he dressed to leave for the office, he took you in his arms, and lied. "It's nothing," he said—of the woman, or of Jenny's headaches? But the headaches continued, and then came the buildup of spinal fluid from Jenny's last craniotomy, forming a golf ball-sized pouch on the back of her head. You called Dr. Morse, who told you to pack for the hospital, for the third time. You waited for Joe. He was late again.

Three hours have passed. Dr. Morse comes out of surgery, his mask, hanging around his neck. He looks over his glasses, which have slipped down his nose. "We did the spinal tap before we opened her up again." And then, the same thing he said before: "I think we've gotten it all this time."

You and Joe move to intensive care. Jenny stirs. Joe presses for the nurse. When she answers, he says, "My child is in pain!" The nurse says it's too soon for more medication.

All Jenny wants is to be touched. You know it because of all that has gone before; you've learned to read her face. You rub the back of her small hand. She grips your fingers and encloses the tips like she did the first time you held her. You remember her tiny newborn head, as bald then as now.

How long was the thing there? How did it creep in without your knowledge? Someone's responsible; someone should pay. You want to hear Joe say, again, that Jenny will be fine. You want to hear him say, again, that he's sorry, that it was only twice and for God's sake, the woman is his boss—what the hell was he supposed to do when she jumped him? He's made it clear to her: never again. Whether or not you believe him, you want to hear all that. Mostly you want to hear what he doesn't say, that he loves you. But he only wraps his arms around his heart.

There is silence in intensive care until the nurse's voice fills the room. Papers are incomplete, she says, so you go to the desk. On your way, you pass the room next door. Behind its glass, a woman lies in her bed. A nurse, standing in the open door, tells an orderly that it's Mrs. Alverson's third time in intensive care, and that she's in critical condition. In the last six hours, the hospital spent another forty thousand dollars on her, and the family can't afford to throw away that kind of money. The nurse says Mrs. Alverson won't make it, so they might as well quit trying. The nurse says she's read the statistics.

You want to tell the nurse that nobody's a statistic; they make it all up. But you're not sure if that's true. You detach yourself from Mrs. Alverson; she is not your responsibility. Still, you're afraid of her death, afraid of any ending. The third time isn't always the charm.

You go back into the room after the papers are complete. You look at Joe; he looks away. He reminds you that tomorrow he will leave. He has a job to do, lots of expenses to pay for. Everything necessary will be done in intensive care, he says; it is fine-tuned. He begins to use corporate-speak. Treating abnormal behaviors of the brain or heart are specialized procedures. Disruption of any lifeline will be signaled to those responsible. Already, his voice seems far away.

Through the walls you hear Mr. Alverson talking to his wife. His voice rolls deep, a one-sided conversation of muffled words like a litany of sins from the confessional. You think of Joe, not so long ago, whispering in your ear when he had no sin to confess.

Mrs. Alverson's family come to offer their blood. One by one, her husband greets them in the doorway, his eyes puffed and gray as rain-soaked cotton. His right arm is bent at the elbow, held up by his left hand, his fingers stroking the side of his face like Jay Leno waiting on a laugh. But this is a place where smiles are stuck on like Band-Aids.

Like Joe, Mr. Alverson is a tall man. He towers over the small nurse who has come to speak to him, yet he appears smaller than she is. He wants the nurse to turn his wife onto her side. He wants the nurse to rub his wife's back because his wife seems uncomfortable in the position she's been in for so long. He crouches when he asks the small nurse to take over his large responsibility.

Joe stands stiffly across the room, watching Jenny. One corner of his mouth looks numbed like a Novocain fix, the other side twitches. You think he might cry.

You see your own reflection in the glass wall of the room, a vague outline holding on to a frail little figure attached to half a dozen fuzzy lines. Then the nurse at the busy nucleus of intensive care flips off the daytime lights because it is ten o'clock. The outlines disappear.

Mr. Alverson and his family sleep on the floor and sofas of the waiting room just outside intensive care. Hour after hour, each makes a thirty-minute vigil like team members in a relay contest, their faces fearful, as if someone might call a halt and tell them the contest is over.

An old man in a straw hat replaces a freckled-face teen in a Katy Perry T-shirt, who replaces a young woman in sandals with a baby on her hip. She presses her face into Mr. Alverson's chest as she leaves, centered between the stained armpits of his plaid work shirt. She kisses him there because she cannot reach his blank Jay Leno face. It's your turn, Daddy, she says, passing on the baton of responsibility.

Jenny wakes, irritated by the IV. She tries to pull it out, and cries. You kiss her palms as if you could kiss away her pain. You want to hold her in your arms but there are too many attachments. She cries again.

Joe presses for the nurse. When she comes, you sit in the chair and order her to put Jenny on your lap. The nurse says it's not standard procedure for intensive-care patients. Joe says the nurse is probably right; it is not a good idea. You tell Joe to go to hell.

All right, the nurse says, then she and Joe lift Jenny onto your lap, untangling the IVs like strings on a marionette.

Jenny stops crying. Joe bends to kiss her and she smiles. Then he leans toward you. "Forgive me," he says. But is it enough?

You turn your face. His mouth misses yours. You miss Joe.

Mr. Alverson comes from his wife's room, his arms set apart from his body as rigidly as those of a Ken doll. Moving to the swarming nucleus of intensive care, he fingers some papers on the counter to get the attention of a small, busy nurse. I think I saw my wife move, he says when she looks up.

At once, she presses a button, and then steps toward Mrs. Alverson's room, while Mr. Alverson pushes open the swinging doors to the waiting area. A baby shrieks as the young woman rushes through, followed by the freckle-faced girl holding on to the old man in the straw hat. They parade, one by one, behind the glass to connect with Mrs. Alverson. Mr. Alverson slides the transparent door closed, shutting them in.

You are shut in, too, connected to Jenny in your lap. Joe is across the room, connected to no one because he defected, because he betrayed. You are weary of his distance, but not tired enough of your pride.

The nurse comes back to resituate Jenny in the bed. She says if all goes well tomorrow, Dr. Morse will probably let her go home the next day. Joe gives a smile of relief, as if the charm has worked.

But you? You can't be sure. You tell Joe that you're going outside. It is too dark, he says, but what he means is, don't leave me in charge. You leave anyway.

You pass Mrs. Alverson's room. The bleep of her monitor becomes a long, strung-out hum. Oh, breathe, Mrs. Alverson, breathe. It's too soon for an ending.

Nurses run past you, and their haste presses you to the wall. Within seconds, one of them is removing the IV. Another is turning off the machines. The old man in the straw hat is wiping his face. The young woman with the baby is bending over Mrs. Alverson, kissing her closed eyes. The freckle-faced girl is tugging Mrs. Alverson's yellow left hand as if she has planned an escape, and if only Mrs. Alverson would come along with her. Mr. Alverson kneels beside the bed of his wife. He buries his face deep into the sheet that covers her. Don't die, he says. You can't die! I haven't told you that I love you!

You push through the swinging doors leading into intensive care and head for the elevator. It takes you down to the main entrance, where you sidestep groups of separated people. Outside, in the artificial light, an old maintenance man is raking dead leaves, making piles of tarnished bronze remnants to load into his waiting truck and carry away. Out of his control and all around him, newly loosened leaves are falling, but he continues to rake through the night shadows, continues to pile, continues to load.

You find a place of distance on the hospital grounds where there's not much light. Like a detached stranger, you stand apart from the maintenance man, the building, and all within it. You look up to the windows on the seventh floor, to intensive care, where Jenny and Joe are waiting. The words of Mr. Alverson wrap like tentacles around your brain and squeeze the hell out of your heart. Whatever his reason, he ought to have known endings come quickly. You ought to know it, too. There is no third-time charm, no taking for granted, and no easy endurance. There is only love in its purest form. Self-sacrificing. Demanding. Forgiving. But can you handle that?

For close to an hour, you debate with yourself, assessing what has gone before, imagining what might come after.

Then you walk back toward the hospital entrance. As you pass close to him, the maintenance man is lifting a load of leaves into the back of his truck. "You reckon I'll ever get done with these?" he asks, smiling as if he's known you all his life.

You don't want to be rude. You answer as cheerfully as you can: "I doubt there's an ending to it."

He laughs as if you've told a joke. "No, ma'am. Sure ain't no ending, just a lot of beginning. Over and over again."

In the glass doors, your reflection and that of the old man twist into one. The reflected face is his but the hand that holds the rake is yours.

You take the elevator to intensive care and pass Mrs. Alverson's room. It is empty now, ready for the next patient.

You are not first, or last, but only next in the relay of life. And its prize is everything that hangs in the balance of intensive care. Now is your turn to carry the baton, certainly for Jenny, and maybe even for Joe.

Near Miss

Mathew Zimmerer

Joey usually slept better than Tess. Or at least that's the way it used to be. It used to be that he would slip easily, when desired, into deep sleep and stir again only with the alarm clock a good eight or nine hours later. "I can sleep through an earthquake," he used to say with a good-natured smile. "Somebody's got a clean conscience," others would note.

Those nights he read before sleeping, he couldn't understand why Tess couldn't simply drift away when his lamp was on. He had no problem doing so when the shoe was on the other foot—though to be honest, it hardly ever was. Years before, they'd tried a clip-on plastic device called a Teeny Weeny Book Light. But when its glare still kept Tess awake, they'd jettisoned that idea.

Snacks in bed were another issue. On the edge of much-coveted slumber, Tess would open one blue eye and groan with humorous disbelief as Joey tried to eat a carrot or celery quietly. His clumsy slow-motion attempts served only to extend the agony, like a crinkly wrapper in a quiet theater. She'd drawn the line, giggling though exhausted, at chips and salsa, and Joey had tried to choose late-night snacks that were less audible.

Things were a little different when the kids were babies. True, Joey wouldn't spring instantly awake at the first peep—Tess would like a light switch—but he would, at last, stir to their noises, and to the palpable agitation of his wife. But he was better at waiting out the fussing and the crying. When Tess would ask if he was awake, his long pauses before answering almost always resulted in her getting up to take care of things.

Now that the kids were older and Tess and Joey were in their forties, they were awakened by other phenomena. While Tess's bladder had never been high capacity, Joey, too, now had to interrupt those previously effortless hours with at least one trip to the bathroom.

This dark morning, he shuffled under the covers and sighed. He still valued his sleep and always had to convince himself to get up and relieve himself after exhausting other options that played out groggily in his thoughts, things like to-do lists for the college, or well-composed replies to his arguments with Gerry. Joey chuckled to himself at the thought of his friend. Part-time yoga instructor, former professor, owner of a money-losing picture-frame shop, Gerry could project an Eastern tranquillity or an East Coast brashness, either image only a glimpse of the complete picture.

Silent Hail Marys meandered through Joey's mind with little effort, like white noise from the TV. A dream had awakened him—at least he thought it had—and it slipped around mysteriously inside him. He considered getting up to write it down, as he'd heard people did. But the idea was only a passing thought.

With an isolated effort, Joey lifted his head, reached up to flip the pillow over and let it fall again with a grunt. It was a little cooler on the back of his neck, but not by much. Last night he'd set the thermostat at 77. Tomorrow, he decided, he'd try 76, although that seemed pretty low for May in Arizona, especially when they still needed more attic insulation.

Tess stirred next to him, and he turned his head to the clock. Another hour and a half before he had to get up, if he could only be still and recapture drowsiness. He focused on his breathing, on the air moving in and out of his body. Gerry and he had been talking about breathing lately, about being in the moment. Joey remembered a Zen story he'd once read on a calendar in Gerry's shop: "365 Days of Zen." He had a flashing image of himself walking through jungle mist toward a pagoda to receive the tale from a serene man in saffron robes. The man, who was bald, didn't speak, but smiled dimly, and Joey saw this man's story in his mind's eye.

The bald man was being chased by a tiger toward an immense chasm and had no choice but to climb down over the edge of the cliff on a vine while the tiger waited ravenously above. As he hung there, suspended between certain death both above and below, the vine began to slip from its hold in the rock face. Just as he was about to plummet to the jagged rocks below, he noticed a splash of red growing in the cliff wall and reached out his hand.

Fresh strawberries.

It was a great story. Gerry liked it too. He said he shared it with his yoga students to help them let go of worries and live in the moment. Joey tried to picture Gerry in the story instead of the monk, with his beard, his ponytail, and his glasses. It kind of worked until the vine started to slip—and Gerry's panic elevated the comical past the transcendent.

Tess shifted again, and he wondered how awake she might be. He rolled over to spoon with her and ran his hand smoothly over her warm hip. If they were both awake, maybe they could get tired again together.

She sighed deeply, then suddenly put out into the darkness, like a word balloon: "Joey, I think I'm pregnant."

His pause and his stillness composed another word balloon for an instant, an empty one. He saw himself as a line drawing in a comic strip, mouth open, exclamation mark above his head, before he moved on to the next panel and said, "When? How could that be?"

"I don't know. The last time. A couple of weeks ago."

She sounded more tired than irritated, or at least more irritated that this revelation was keeping her awake than at the revelation itself, although Joey knew her alarm was greater than his own. As she got up to go to the bathroom, Joey rolled carefully onto his back and listened.

He felt guilty, mostly. Shortly after Michael was born, Tess had gotten up from the hospital bed to go to the bathroom and fainted on the toilet. Joey'd been leaning against the door joking with her when she slumped like a rag doll. He'd rushed forward to catch her and then had her limp form wrestled away by a nurse who'd entered with impeccable timing. This pushy nurse had gotten her back to bed while he hovered to help. The nurse's attitude had made him wonder if he was violating some institutional protocol. Or maybe she'd just thought he was a careless jerk. He felt the same guilt now, like he should have known that the loss of blood during the birth had left her weak, like he should have kept an arm around her and taken care of her—like he had let his self-centered unawareness endanger his wife.

This memory led to others. He remembered the night when the terms "placenta previa" and "bed rest" and "ten percent of cases" had all coalesced into reality as he listened to the *chop chop chop* of a helicopter and watched Tess fly away from their local hospital to St. Joseph's downtown, its facilities better equipped to handle the younger preemies. A helicopter. That had been Esther's first flight, though she wouldn't be born, via cesarean section, for another month while Tess mostly lay on her back in the quiet wing of the birth floor. Joey still felt like he had to defend himself, good-naturedly, for his ignorance about the seriousness of the condition: "They lulled me into a false sense of security. They mentioned it only in passing. I thought they'd give her some pills and send her back home." Ten percent of cases. They never said anything about how serious it could be if you were among those ten percent.

Luke was born last. Emergency C-section. Near rupture of the uterus. The complications were quite unexpected this time. Dr. Ewing had said this didn't mean Tess couldn't have more babies, but both Joey and Tess were satisfied with their little family. Three was, for them, a charm.

Nana, Tess's mom, was a little more to the point. One Thanksgiving Joey had asked about her new piece of coffee-table art, a greenish-metal Native American sculpture of abstract figures dancing in a circle. "It's a fertility dance," Nana had said, "You keep away from that," and maneuvered him toward the Texas sheet cake.

Tess came back into the bedroom, pushed aside the drape, and looked out. A dim white light cast itself into the room. As if on cue, a couple of birds chattered outside the window. She turned to Joey with a look of self-conscious expectation. Under the covers, matching her self-consciousness, he offered, "Should you have started by now?"

"I think so. I don't know. I don't know what my body's doing."

Tess said this at times. It was somewhat ironic. She probably had a better idea of what her body was doing than did many other women. She usually knew where she was in her fertility cycle within a day or two. In those first years of marriage, this meant waking up early to chart her body temperature and checking other signs. It had been like a science project. Back then Joey would often slip his arm around Tess and whisper, "Want to do an experiment?" Tess had put a playful foot down when he'd begun referring to their bedroom as "the lab."

Tess had been on the pill at first, the same as most women, if the surveys Joey'd read were true. But the alternate idea had soon been introduced—by Ron and Mona, of all people, friends they'd gone to school with in Flagstaff. Like Gerry, Ron and Mona weren't religious. They did their shopping at organic-food stores and wore a lot of knit clothing. After college, they quickly left behind the tract homes and fences of Phoenix for the unconfined forests of Eugene, Oregon. Joey and Tess had made the trek to visit. He remembered playing Yahtzee on their deck, wet with rain, and drinking wine, and talking about spirituality and sex and babies. No artificial birth control for Ron and Mona, but no disposition toward any particular faith structure either. Just the desire to be natural instead of pumping the body full of false hormones.

Some couples trying to get pregnant used the information they gathered to time their conjugal union to the day, and even the time of day, when the woman was most fertile.

Tess and Joey had never required such precision.

Thus, it was only somewhat ironic that Tess would plead ignorance of her body's behavior. As she aged and changed, her body behaved differently, and it was aggravating for Tess to be uncertain, not to have better control, especially with an amorous husband eagerly waiting for her to give the word.

"I bet you're just late," he said, attempting a balance between sensitivity and blithe assurance. "It doesn't seem like it's been that long."

She gave a mild groan. "Ooh . . ." It was her "I really want to sleep and can't" groan. "I think I'm just gonna shower," she said, and stood with one hand on the sill, contemplating this weighty decision.

Joey looked at the digital clock on the nightstand. 5:20. "Is Fry's open?"

She looked at him hopefully. "It should be."

"Why don't I go get a pregnancy test? Then you won't have to wonder about it. At least we'll know."

Tess made a cute face, even in the tension of the moment performing for half a beat like a lost waif. "Would you do that for me?"

She knew he would, of course. It made Joey smile that she would dare to be light. He knew very well the extent of her worry.

As he drove to the store, the worry came along for the ride. It wasn't just the likelihood of complications with the pregnancy, though of course that was the paramount fear. Things were so different now, so complete in their way. The kids were older, Luke almost in junior high. Tess had been in her new job at the university for three years. They'd accept the child and love it, of course—he shuddered as he thought of other popular options—but life would be different. If Tess was pregnant, her hours would have to be cut back. Her doctorate would have to be put on hold. He'd have to come home early from work. They'd be on the verge of retirement when this kid graduated from high school.

A dean at Joey's college had divorced and then married a younger woman. He was nearing sixty and had a four-year-old daughter. Joey and Tess wouldn't be far behind. All those diapers and bottles and the potty training. Sleepless nights. Starting school. They often joked that if they had to go back and do it all over again—meeting and marrying and raising a family—they wouldn't have the energy. And now they might have to find a little extra.

As he turned right onto the main thoroughfare, the sun was blinding. It illuminated every spot of grime on the windshield, but the road, cars, and traffic signals beyond were another matter. The cars had become vague and polished gleams of light, dashing and slashing in confusion like blazing swords. Unable to see a thing, Joey was driving by trust. Nervous, he slowed for a stoplight. Luke's name, hastily smeared backwards above the parking sticker in the far lower corner, eagerly sought his approval until a merciful left-turn arrow provided an exit from the dazzle.

There was an Ace Hardware store in the strip mall next to Fry's, and it reminded him of his dream. Tools left out in the rain—that had been one part of it. The shed—an older outbuilding, nothing like their storage room off the garage—was open but difficult to get to. It was grown over with long thorny vines, woody vines, like the pink-flowered branches that stuck out from their desert plants out front. In the dream he was late for work but had to get into the shed for some reason. Dozens of tools littered the lawn. He had to choose among rusty hedge trimmers, tin snips, and bolt cutters to cut back the thorns and get to the shed.

As he lurched to a stop in the store parking lot, he breathed deep and exhaled, squeezed his eyes shut and then opened them wide again. Lack of sleep would catch up with him later. He'd need to move through the store quickly—not something he was particularly good at. His tendency was to start with a hand basket, load it up, then return to the front for a cart anyway, basket heavy with goods on one arm, watermelon under the other, milk jug hanging by two fingers. No time for that this morning. Just the pregnancy test. Although . . . He may as well get doughnuts for the kids. And some prepackaged lunches. That would save Tess having to mess with any meals this morning.

He moved through the automatic door at a pretty quick pace, sporting deck shoes with no socks, green checked pajama pants, and an old golf hat. Swinging his elbows, he veered to the right, toward pharmaceuticals. Aisle 14. Parallel ranks of athletic tape, deodorant, and dental floss stood at attention as he cruised by. Tissue, feminine napkins . . . pregnancy tests—there they were, stored for sale behind a glass case. He placed his fingers in the indentation of the sliding glass door and pulled. Locked up. Like cigarettes and razor blades.

He stood tall and let his head pivot in the universal signal for "customer assistance needed." But there was no one near, only distant sounds of refrigeration equipment humming, and cardboard being cut. High above the aisle at one end hovered a large disk of a mirror, like a flying saucer tilted for takeoff. "Heading back to the mothership?" Joey wondered. Other than his own gawking image near the bottom, this envoy from beyond showed signs of only distant movement.

Well, then, doughnuts and lunch first. And maybe a little something or other for Tess.

He got both chocolate and powdered mini doughnuts in waxed cardboard boxes. The lunches came in sterile rectangles of plastic: processed meat in uniform shapes, cheese, crackers, small individually wrapped snacks, and transparent pouches of dark juice that looked like bags of sticky blood.

Smiling, Joey took a quick detour from the refrigerated deli section through produce. He may as well get some fruit to go with the doughnuts. The cantaloupe looked better than the grapes, he thought, and he selected one, hefting it thoughtfully in his hand.

Okay, enough already. Get going.

His self-chastisement was cut short by a shiny mound of red and yellow. Queen Anne cherries. Tess's favorite. She'd fallen in love with them during that visit to Ron and Mona's in Eugene, eating them right off the tree in their backyard. Six ninety-nine a pound, but what did that matter? She could use a little something today. And if the results were positive, she could definitely use a little something today.

He piled his other items onto a scale and scooped several pounds of cherries into a plastic bag, their smooth round skin like cool leather to his touch. Then, bag in hand, he tried to clamp the lunch boxes under his arm and balance the doughnuts on top . . . He had to leave one hand free for the cantaloupe. *Geez, maybe I do need a cart.* He spotted a basket someone had abandoned by the florist stand, and he adopted it for the trip back to aisle 14. As he dumped his goods into the basket, he inhaled the fragrance of roses, cool and wet as they waited in their tilted buckets, pink and yellow and red. Flowers would be nice, but he hurried himself along before he could consider them further.

He approached the aisle now—basket with lunches, doughnuts, and cherries in one hand, cantaloupe like a tan shot put in the other—but he stopped short partway down. An employee fussed in the aisle, a white-haired woman in a blue-and-white synthetic vest with a ring of keys on her hip. Joey suddenly felt the awkwardness of a teenager in the dirty-magazine section. Or as if he had just disrobed for an examination while a doctor snapped on a latex glove. Good lord. He was forty-five. He had three kids. Why this sudden bout of modesty? He looked up at her reflection in the convex mirror. *What news from the mothership?* She looked up too, then turned gently to face him.

"Can I help you find anything?"

She was smiling. It was a nice smile.

"Are these the pregnancy tests?" he asked after a nervous pause, pointing at the glass case he'd earlier found unassailable.

The white-haired woman practically lit up. There were several kinds, and they were right here, and let her open this for him. "They go from least expensive to most expensive, right to left," she said, looking up at him from where she knelt on one knee, her keen blue eyes assuring him that she would not abandon him in this hour of need. Joey leaned near her toward the case. She smelled like Ivory Soap. She smiled even more reassuringly, and he couldn't help but smile himself. He wondered if she might hug him.

It was more than good customer service. She was sharing in the good news like a mother's friend, a beloved aunt, like a wealthy relative at a baby shower. No longer was he middle aged and sneaking in to cover up something. He was an innocent again. It was a joyful announcement now, an annunciation. Joey was the lucky guy whose wife was going to have a baby. He took his time choosing the highest-priced option—the one on the left. Nothing too good for his wife. He even contemplated asking the woman to unlock the cigar case, as a joke, but thanked her with good feeling instead.

At the checkout line, glossy cleavage and hot sex secrets clashed glaringly with the Frank Capra charm of aisle 14. From wire racks, the headlines appealed to women with never-ending streams of advice about how to please their men. "Advice from our experts!" "Hot new tips!" "The dirty things he really wants you to do!" A series of sacramental confessions processed through Joey's memory. The Indian priest in San Diego, the old priest in Tucson, and several of those in his more immediate vicinity, their advice about Joey's sins more eclectic than he would have liked, seemed to join calm forces here at the register to shelter him from the bombardment, absolve him of excessive pop-culture entanglement, and guide him back to the matter at hand.

Also helping was a pink ribbon for breast cancer awareness pinned to a murky plastic cylinder half filled with coins. It spoke to Joey of hospitals and emergencies. Luke's C-section and Esther's helicopter seemed to rattle down the conveyor belt with the groceries, and Joey's pulse rattled along with them. It had been eleven years since the most dangerous situation. How would a pregnancy affect Tess's health now?

Walking to the car, Joey imagined a bespectacled woman, some nameless ideologue conjured, perhaps, from the editorial pages of those magazines, following him. As he tossed the plastic bags onto the passenger seat, she climbed in the back to harangue him about his wife's health. What was the Hemingway story about hills and white elephants? The one where the callous traveler tries to convince his pregnant female companion to have the simple operation and "let the air in"? Joey was the callous traveler, but his solipsism lay in unquestionably wanting the child.

The phantom in the backseat rolled her eyes at the idea, leaned forward, and lectured him about his driving and about the high risks of pregnancy for women after age forty-five. He saw himself nervously checking his blind spots and helplessly nodding to the rearview mirror, hoping to prove somehow through his bumbling humility that he did care about his wife. Then, in the seat beside him he pictured the white-haired lady from aisle 14. She held the doughnuts in her lap and smiled as if she and Joey were in on a joke the woman in the backseat was excluded from.

He turned left a street early and went by Holy Rosary. The stained glass was dull on the outside, and he wished he had time to stop in for a visit. He pictured Tess sitting alone in a front pew in an amber glow, gently caressing her own stomach under a watchful icon of Our Lady.

As he made the sign of the cross, Joey's dream flashed into his mind again. It was an earlier part of the dream. He was late for work but had to go into the backyard. He went out in his boxers and noticed it had rained heavily through the night. Tess and the kids had draped all the sleeping bags and quilts over the block-wall fence. They were dripping with rainwater. That's when he noticed the tools rusting on the ground among the thorns. That's why he needed to get to the shed, he remembered, to put away the tools. But the thorns blocked his way.

The dream dissipated as his tires rolled across a patch of gravel near their driveway, bringing him back to the moment and pulling him and his purchases into the garage. He wondered if any of the kids would be out of bed.

Tess was in the kitchen now, showered, skin shining, hair wet, eyes still tired. He showed her the breakfast and lunch groceries, and she attempted a smile as her glance went to the other bag.

"Kids awake?" he whispered.

"I don't think so," she said as he gave her the bag. Joey followed her back to the master bedroom, keeping the cherries half behind his back as a surprise. He listened to her tear open the cardboard package in the bathroom, noticed the soft crackle of the instructions, sat on the bed with the cherries in his lap, and waited.

A brood of his sod-busting antecedents beckoned from a dusty black-and-white photo on a dusty dresser. Patriarch and matriarch sat collapsed on chairs with a dozen of their progeny piled about them. The entire clan stared into the camera a bit stunned, it seemed, in their ill-fitting white dresses and black suits. A gilt rope snaked its way around the frame. An unseen child in the photo would fall just short of being born and precipitate the death of the mother. The solemn line of the woman's mouth seemed to signal a steely resignation to her fate. The father, Joey's great-grandfather, would never forgive himself. Though the tragedy lay months ahead as the grandfather sat for this family portrait, Joey wondered if under the dust of the years, under the exhaustion of the prairie, it was guilt he saw in his ancestor's eyes. He was suddenly terrified, and a prayer—involuntary, earnest—welled up from within. "Dear God, no. Nothing like that, Jesus. Please."

Then came the dream again.

In the dream he was worried. The tools were rusted. The shed was unapproachable. The thorns choked all the possibilities. The gas meter—painted fire-engine red, he now remembered, with its valve pinched through like modeling clay—was hissing. He observed, in his dream, that the gas leak shouldn't be making any noise. *That was the great danger, wasn't it? That you didn't notice any sound? No . . . that wasn't right. It was the smell you didn't notice, yes? Or noticed only because they'd added some odor to it, since natural gas didn't have any odor?* He was confused and groggy. He needed to go to work. He didn't have time to take care of this. Yet there it hissed.

And then Joey recalled the most disconcerting part of the dream. He realized as he was dreaming that his alarm was not nearly great enough. He was prepared to leave the catastrophe till later. He would rush off to work and leave it all for Tess.

It was a careless thought in the dream, something tossed away. But awake now, Joey's breath came in quick, guilty gasps. Leave it all for Tess . . .

Joey envisioned a child carrier in the backseat of the car, complete with a fourth addition, a baby girl in pink. Tess sat on one side talking to the child in a high, lovely voice. On the other side sat the female specter with an expression of distaste. In the passenger seat, Joey's friend Gerry made a surprise appearance, his glasses focused on the road, his expression inscrutable.

What would he think of Tess and Joey having another child? Joey's worries expanded from Tess and her body, warm and near in the bathroom, to larger concerns, coldly abstract and frightening in their gravity. His friend would never overtly criticize him and Tess—he was often complimentary about their parenting—but even those compliments seemed to emphasize that most other parents weren't worthy of children, and no one was really worthy of very many. Gerry made veiled comments, sometimes, about large families. He'd borrowed an ongoing joke from a Monty Python movie: "Bloody Catholics, filling the bloody world up with bloody people." Joey seldom took offense. He'd usually just laugh, which was what he thought Gerry mainly wanted.

He breathed deeply, closed his eyes, and exhaled slowly.

He thought of Ron and Mona, up in Eugene, practicing yoga and drinking herbal tea. Gerry would like Ron and Mona. Wouldn't it have been cool if Gerry had been there on their deck that day so many children ago, drinking wine under the rain clouds? That day when they'd teased Tess and Joey about a fertility practice that dangled, theologically speaking, right in their own backyard? Sure, he and Tess had stumbled at times and struggled to make sense of it all, sometimes even more as they got older and more tired. But in his better moments, Joey felt peace and self-discipline, and, more than that, a resonating awareness of design and meaning in the world, an impulse to let go of worry and excessive planning and open himself to possibilities.

Tess had experienced those medical complications, of course. That essential fact and its accompanying fears could not be changed. But that fact did not, by any means, constitute a foregone conclusion. And what if, he considered, what if that fact were different? Who knew what tomorrow might hold?

Once, on a cross-country vacation, they'd taken a last-minute side trip to an amusement park. Joey had a very clear memory of Tess in pink tennis shoes, neon green shorts, and gigantic tortoiseshell sunglasses running ahead of him and the kids to be first in line for a roller coaster. She was looking back over her shoulder, waving her hands in "hurry-up" gestures, and laughing. . . . This was what life was all about, this openness to opportunity. Was the world big enough to support more of this? Did he and Tess have enough love to share with another?

Joey turned his head to the bedroom window. Though the day looked to be quite warm and sunny, he pictured mammals in snowy regions moving instinctively into the darkness, settling in, accepting the timing of the universe.

"Joey . . ."

She didn't know yet. He could tell when he walked in, her blue eyes burdened with apprehension. "Will you look with me?" He nodded, and she showed it to him, a long piece of plastic, like a space-age thermometer, with a small oval portal to the future. She grabbed his hand and took a deep breath, then held it up as the two of them leaned their heads together to see.

A lone dash of red.

Negative.

The tension drained from his wife's body as if forming a puddle at their feet. The air itself was more relaxed. Joey smiled. He was glad for her.

What a morning.

All that worry and now life could roll along as it had been. Roll along as it had.

Joey sighed.

But he wondered, too . . .

What if . . . what if we could let ourselves plummet off the cliff a little? Just a little?

Tess put her hands on his chest and looked up at him. "Thanks for going to the store for me, Joey." He smiled and kissed her, then started to take his clothes off to shower before work. The plastic-and-chrome dial of the shower faucet, cool and wet in his hand, seemed like a seashell as he turned it and opened the valve. Over the sound of the water, he heard Tess rustling in the other room and then an exclamation tinged with delight.

"What are these?"

He leaned out of the bathroom door, underplaying it.

"Oh, did you see those? I thought you might like them."

"You got cherries for me?" She said it like the innocent waif again, cradling them up near her face as she would a lost puppy, and he laughed. She knew he loved that.

"Dad, look at this! Hurry!"

Michael was up and must have heard them. Joey put his pajama bottoms back on and left the water running to go see his oldest son standing at the back patio door, shirtless, his wavy hair sticking out in different directions. Joey looked through the window of the door and saw the underside of a pink gecko, adhering to the screen by twenty tiny round pads on its toes. "It's eating a little moth," Michael said, and indeed it was, patiently holding the still-fluttering creature in its mouth and occasionally gulping it in a bit more.

"What are you guys looking at?" Luke had joined them and was soon intrigued. "Is that a moth?" This was affirmed with Joey's hand on his shoulder and a nod. Luke's next words were whispered, so as not to disturb the spell: "We should tell Mom." Soon it was the five of them, Esther leaning against her father, wrapped in a fuzzy striped blanket, Luke and Michael huddled on the sides, Tess absentmindedly clutching the bag of cherries.

"Oh my gosh," said Tess, "isn't that interesting?" and she looked at them all with open mouth, a wonderful light in her eyes.

They watched in fascination until the moth was consumed. "I wonder if we can see it moving down into its stomach," said Michael. This seemed reasonable. Geckos, at least the ones on their patio, had a transparent quality. This one reminded Joey of the dark pink and flesh-toned pictures he'd seen of human beings inside the womb. He leaned in to look at its dark eyes, distant water sounds trickling from his waiting shower. The kids soon discovered the cherries, and they all stood watching through the window, silently eating the fruit, spitting the pits into their cupped hands.

About the Authors

 KAREN BRITTEN, the author of "Eyes That Pour Forth," is the first-place winner of the 2012 Tuscany Prize for Catholic Fiction—Short Story category. She is a fiction candidate at the University of Florida's MFA program in creative writing. She has a degree in philosophy and religious studies from Auburn University and taught high school theology in Florida for five years. She is a native Californian, but currently lives in the very humid town of Gainesville, Florida.

 MOLLIE FICEK, who earned second place in the 2012 Tuscany Prize for Catholic Fiction—Short Story category for her story "The Reasons Why", hails from the Midwest—the land of hotdish and high winds. She lives in Boise, Idaho, after recently completing her MFA at Boise State University. She has published in *The New Ohio Review* and *The Hawai'i Review*. She is currently at work on her first novel.

KAYE PARK HINCKLEY, third-place winner for "Moon Dance" and honorable mention for "Intensive Care," has a bachelor's degree in fine arts from Spring Hill College, Mobile, Alabama. A former advertising agency owner, her fiction has appeared in several literary journals, most recently *Dappled Things*. She is inspired by her Catholic faith, her family, and a deep connection to the Bible Belt South, where the conversation centers on God and sinners, family and football, and maybe a favorite old hound dog. She lives with her husband in Dothan, Alabama. They have five grown children and nine grandchildren, so far. Tuscany Press will be publishing Ms. Hinckley's first novel, *A Hunger in the Heart,* for spring 2013.

BERNARD SCOTT, who earned fourth place for "True or False," prior to his conversion to the Catholic faith was a Protestant missionary to the artistic community of Greenwich Village. His writing includes published poetry (*First Things, Logos Review, The Wanderer*); feature writing (*The Village Voice; Exodus Quarterly*); an honorary mention in Macmillan's annual *Best Short Stories;* and most recently a Catholic adventure novel. He is also a linguist, having served in the Air Force as a Russian, French, and Vietnamese translator. He is the architect of OpenLogos, an Internet-based, computerized translation system. Other writings and publications of his are available on the website http://www.logosinstitute.org/. He lives in retirement with his wife on the west coast of central Florida.

DR. MICHAEL PIAFSKY, who received fifth place for "Water," is an associate professor and director of the writing program at Spring Hill College, in Mobile, Alabama. His recent fiction and nonfiction appeared in *The Missouri Review, jabberwocky review, Ocho, Meridian, Bar Stories,* and elsewhere. Earlier this year he was a finalist in the *Glimmer Train* Short Story Award for New Writers.

L. C. RICARDO, an honorable mention winner for "The Debt," has a master's in Arthurian Literature and an insatiable wanderlust. She is a mom and aspiring writer living in Florida, and is loyal to the Holy Father and the Magisterium. Her favorite writers, from whom she draws armfuls of inspiration, are G. K. Chesterton, Emily Dickinson, C. S. Lewis, David Jones, J. R. R. Tolkien, and Flannery O'Connor. She blogs regularly about fairy tales and storytelling on Spinning Straw into Gold (http://spinstrawintogold.blogspot.com) and hopes some day to own a spinning wheel and to visit Norway.

CAROLINE VALENCIA-DALISAY, the author of "Excess Baggage," which earned an honorable mention, is from the Philippines and moved to the United States as a teenager. She is deeply interested in the cultural wealth of immigrants, and in the challenges immigrants face. She is a cradle Catholic and her writing is generously flavored with the Catholic faith. Her writing has appeared in a number of small journals and an anthology of her poetry is available at http://ofliliesandsparrows.blogspot.com/.

S. L. SCOTT, who received an honorable mention for "The Morning Star," is a native of St. Louis, Missouri. She is currently a graduate assistant at Southeast Missouri State University and is pursuing her master's degree in professional writing and publishing. She has been published in *Journey* magazine and was a co-editor of *Big Muddy* literary magazine.

MATHEW ZIMMERER recevied an honorable mention for "Near Miss." He grew up in a trailer house behind his parents' bar, restaurant, and dinner theater on the edge of a wheat field near Billings, Montana. He graduated with a BS in theater from Northern Arizona University in Flagstaff where he and his future wife met as singing waiters. He acts professionally on occasion, has a master's degree in education, and teaches high school English in Chandler, Arizona, where he lives with his wife and four sons.

2012 TUSCANY PRIZE FOR CATHOLIC FICTION

NOVEL

Wild Spirits
By Pita Okute

NOVELLA

The Book of Jotham
By Arthur Powers